Where Shadows Dwell: A Tale of Love, Danger, and Deception in the Western Frontier

Beate Lang

Published by Beate Lang, 2024.

This is a work of fiction. Similarities to real people, places, or events are entirely coincidental.

WHERE SHADOWS DWELL: A TALE OF LOVE, DANGER, AND DECEPTION IN THE WESTERN FRONTIER

First edition. November 1, 2024.

Copyright © 2024 Beate Lang.

ISBN: 979-8224003723

Written by Beate Lang.

Table of Contents

Chapter 1: The Last Shot 1
Chapter 2: The Stranger in Black 11
Chapter 3: Whispers in the Dark 19
Chapter 4: Dangerous Alliance 25
Chapter 5: Dance with the Devil 31
Chapter 6: Shadows of the Past 37
Chapter 7: Bloody Trails 43
Chapter 8: Betrayal and Loyalty 49
Chapter 9: Storm Over Canyon 55
Chapter 10: Fire and Ice 61
Chapter 11: Dance with Shadows 65
Chapter 12: Bloody Dawn 69
Chapter 13: Ghosts of the Past 73
Chapter 14: Cards Revealed 77
Chapter 15: Before the Storm 81
Chapter 16: Thunder from a Clear Sky 85
Chapter 17: In Fire 91
Chapter 18: Dawn 95

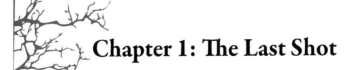

Chapter 1: The Last Shot

The morning sun crept over Shadow Creek like a guilty thief, casting long shadows across the dusty main street. Sheriff Thomas Wilson stood at his office window, coffee cup warming his weathered hands, watching his town wake up. His town. The thought still brought a smile to his face, even after twenty years of wearing the badge.

"Another exciting morning in paradise?" Grace's voice, rich with familiar sarcasm, broke through his contemplation. She leaned against the doorframe, her deputy's badge catching the morning light.

Thomas turned to face his daughter, noting how she unconsciously mirrored his stance – one hand near her holster, weight slightly shifted to the left. Teaching her to shoot had been easier than teaching her to temper that sharp tongue of hers.

"Paradise got a bit more interesting," he said, nodding toward the window. "Railroad men in town."

Grace's green eyes narrowed as she watched a sleek black carriage roll down the street, looking as out of place as a peacock in a chicken coop. "Mr. Harris again?"

"Vincent Harris," Thomas corrected, though they both knew she remembered the name perfectly well. "Seems our friendly railroad representative can't take no for an answer."

"He can't take no for an answer in more ways than one," Grace muttered, unconsciously touching the silver locket at her throat – her mother's last gift.

The memory of Harris's proposal last month still made her skin crawl. He'd arranged everything perfectly: the romantic dinner, the string quartet brought specially from San Francisco, the flash of diamonds that probably cost more than their entire town. Everything except asking what she actually wanted.

"You know," Thomas began carefully, setting down his coffee, "most fathers would be thrilled to have their daughter courted by a man of his position."

Grace snorted. "Most fathers don't teach their daughters to read tracks and shoot straight." She moved to the desk, picking up the morning's wanted posters. "Besides, there's something wrong about a man who smiles without it ever reaching his eyes."

Thomas watched her flip through the posters with practiced efficiency. They'd had this conversation about marriage before, usually ending with Grace comparing potential suitors to various forms of rattlesnakes. But lately, there was an urgency to his concern that Grace couldn't quite understand.

The office door swung open, bringing with it a swirl of dust and Eleanor "Ellie" Martinez's distinctive perfume. The saloon owner's expression was as dark as her eyes.

"Sheriff, we need to talk." Ellie's gaze flickered to Grace. "Privately."

"Whatever you need to say to me, you can say in front of my deputy," Thomas replied, but Grace was already moving toward the door.

"It's fine. I need to check on Sarah anyway. She was acting strange at breakfast." Grace paused at the threshold. "Though when isn't she lately?"

As she stepped onto the boardwalk, the sound of hooves drew her attention. The black carriage had stopped in front of the sheriff's office, and Vincent Harris emerged like a dark prophet, his tailored suit pristine despite the dusty air. His smile, when he spotted her, was perfect. Too perfect.

"Miss Wilson," he tipped his hat. "Looking lovely as ever."

"Mr. Harris," she returned coolly. "Back so soon?"

"Progress waits for no one, my dear." His gray eyes held hers a moment too long. "Though some things are worth waiting for."

Before she could form a suitably cutting reply, Sarah Anderson hurried past, nearly colliding with Harris. The seamstress's face was pale, her usually immaculate hair disheveled.

"Sarah?" Grace called after her friend, but Sarah just shook her head and hurried on.

The morning air suddenly felt heavier, charged with something beyond the usual desert heat. Grace glanced back at the office window where her father's silhouette stood in discussion with Ellie. Something was wrong. She could feel it in her bones, the way her father had taught her to feel an approaching storm.

Speaking of storms...

The wind changed first.

Grace felt it before she saw it – that peculiar stillness that preceded chaos, like the intake of breath before a scream. To the west, the sky turned the color of old brass, a massive wall of dust rolling toward Shadow Creek like nature's own cavalry charge.

"Get inside!" she shouted to the people on the street, her voice carrying the authority of her badge. "Dust storm coming!"

The townsfolk didn't need to be told twice. They'd danced this deadly waltz before. Doors slammed, shutters rattled closed, and the street emptied faster than a saloon during a sermon.

Harris glanced at the approaching storm with aristocratic disdain. "Miss Wilson, please allow me to offer you shelter in my carriage."

"I have duties, Mr. Harris." She gestured to the badge that gleamed against her leather vest. "Your concern is noted but unnecessary."

Inside the sheriff's office, her father and Ellie had moved to the window. Even through the glass, Grace could see the tension in her father's stance. Whatever Ellie had told him had shaken his usual calm.

The first gust hit like a slap, sending tumbleweeds dancing past like drunken dancers. Grace hurried inside, brushing dust from her clothes.

The office was strangely quiet, the usual creaking of the old building muffled by the approaching storm.

"Ellie," her father said, "we'll finish this discussion later. Get back to the saloon before—"

"Before what, Thomas?" Ellie's voice carried an edge Grace had never heard before. "Before it's too late?"

The sheriff's hand went to his gun belt – not grabbing, just resting there. A gesture Grace had seen hundred times when he was troubled. "Grace, escort Ellie back to the saloon."

"I can find my own way," Ellie snapped, but her eyes held something that looked suspiciously like fear. She paused at the door, glancing back. "Just... remember what I said, Thomas. Please."

The storm hit in earnest then, turning the world outside into a sepia nightmare. Wind howled through every crack in the building's weathered boards, and dust filtered in like golden smoke.

"Dad?" Grace moved closer to her father. "What's going on?"

Thomas Wilson looked older suddenly, the lines in his face deeper than they'd been that morning. "Nothing you need to worry about, sweetheart." He forced a smile that didn't reach his eyes – so like Harris in that moment that it made her skin crawl. "Just the usual town business."

A sharp knock at the door made them both jump. Harris stood there, a handkerchief pressed to his face against the dust.

"Sheriff Wilson," his cultured voice barely carried over the storm. "A word, if you please. About our previous discussion."

Her father's hand tightened on his gun belt. "Grace, go check on Doctor Cooper. Make sure he's prepared if anyone gets caught in this storm."

"Dad—"

"That's an order, Deputy."

The formality in his voice stung worse than the flying sand. Grace hesitated, every instinct screaming that something was wrong. But twenty years of obeying that voice won out.

"Yes, sir." She grabbed her duster from the hook, shrugging it on. "I'll be right back."

The last image she had of her father was him standing tall against the storm-darkened window, Harris's shadow stretching across the floor between them like a chasm.

The street had become a horizontal cliff face of stinging sand. Grace pulled her bandana over her nose and mouth, squinting against the maelstrom. The doctor's office was only fifty yards away, but in this storm, it might as well have been miles.

She was halfway there when she heard it.

A gunshot. Muffled by the storm but unmistakable to ears trained from childhood to know the difference between thunder and trouble.

Grace spun, drawing her Colt in the same motion. The storm had thickened to the point where the sheriff's office was just a darker shape in the golden murk. Another shot, or was that just thunder?

"Dad!" Her voice was lost in the howling wind.

She fought her way back, the storm trying to push her sideways with every step. The office door stood open, banging against the wall like an erratic heartbeat.

"Dad? Mr. Harris?"

No answer.

Her boots left dusty prints on the floor as she entered, gun first like he'd taught her. The office was empty, but the back door that led to the cells swung gently in the wind.

The figure on the floor behind the desk wasn't moving.

"No," she whispered. "No, no, no..."

She knew it was him before she reached him. Knew it from the badge that caught the dim light, from the familiar boots, from the gun still in its holster.

Sheriff Thomas Wilson lay face-down in a spreading pool of darkness that the storm's light painted almost black. Grace fell to her knees beside him, fingers searching desperately for a pulse even as her mind registered details with cruel clarity: powder burns on his shirt, the angle of the wound, the way his hand was stretched out toward something she couldn't see.

"Help!" She screamed into the storm. "Somebody help!"

But the wind stole her words, and the dust kept falling, and somewhere in Shadow Creek, a killer walked free, sheltered by the same storm that had hidden their crime.

Grace Wilson knelt in her father's blood and made two promises: one to the badge that now lay heavy against her heart, and one to the memory of the man who'd taught her to wear it.

Justice and vengeance. Sometimes, they were the same thing.

The storm was already beginning to settle when Doctor James Cooper burst through the door, his medical bag clutched in white-knuckled hands. He took in the scene with the rapid assessment of a battlefield surgeon: the blood, the body, the deputy's drawn gun.

"Grace," he said softly, as if speaking to a spooked horse. "Let me see him."

She hadn't realized she was still pointing her Colt at the door. Lowering it slowly, she watched as Cooper knelt beside her father, his movements quick and professional. But there was something in his eyes – a flash of... what? Resignation? Recognition?

"Did you see anyone?" she demanded. "In the street, during the storm?"

"Only shadows." His hands moved over her father's body with practiced efficiency. "The dust was too thick. Though I thought I heard a carriage..."

Harris's carriage. Grace's mind latched onto the detail like a drowning woman grabbing rope. "Harris was here. He wanted to talk to Dad."

"Vincent Harris?" Cooper's hands stilled for just a moment. "Interesting timing."

Before she could question that particular emphasis, Ellie burst in, bringing the scent of dust and whiskey with her. Her dark eyes widened at the scene, but Grace caught something else in her expression – not surprise, but a grim confirmation.

"Dios mío," Ellie whispered, crossing herself. Then, sharper: "Doctor Cooper, we need to move him. Now."

"He's my father," Grace started to protest, but Cooper was already nodding.

"The undertaker's is closer than my office," he said. "And more private. Grace, I need you to—"

"I'm not leaving him."

"No." Something passed between Cooper and Ellie – quick as a card shark's shuffle, but Grace caught it. "But you need to find Harris. He was the last person to see your father alive. That makes him—"

"My first suspect." Grace stood, her knees protesting the movement. She looked down at her blood-stained hands and felt a laugh bubble up – harsh and wild as a coyote's cry. "Dad always said I was a better tracker than deputy."

"Grace," Ellie stepped forward, "maybe you should wait—"

"For what?" The words came out sharp as brass shell casings. "For the killer to skip town? For more 'progress' to roll through and bury the truth like this storm buried our streets?" She checked her gun with mechanical precision. "Dad taught me everything about being a lawman except how to bury him."

"At least let me clean you up first," Cooper offered, but Grace was already moving toward the door.

"Later. Right now, I need to—"

A movement caught her eye. Sarah stood in the doorway, her face as white as laundry on a line. Their eyes met, and for a moment, Grace saw naked fear in her friend's expression.

"I heard..." Sarah's voice cracked. "Grace, I'm so sorry. I should have..."

Should have what? But Sarah just shook her head and backed away, disappearing into the settling dust like a ghost at sunrise.

Grace filed the reaction away – another piece to a puzzle she couldn't quite see yet. Right now, she had a suspect to find and a badge to honor. The weight of it felt strange against her chest, heavier than it had any right to be.

"Doctor Cooper," she said without turning around, "take care of him. Ellie, I'll need statements from everyone in the saloon, especially anyone who left during the storm."

"Of course," Ellie replied, too quickly. "Anything you need."

Grace stepped out into the aftermath of the storm. The street lay under a fresh blanket of dust, pristine except for a single set of carriage tracks leading west. She touched her mother's locket, remembering the last time she'd seen her father smile – just that morning, watching his town wake up.

Some part of her knew that when she found Harris, when she learned the truth, nothing would ever be the same. Shadow Creek had changed in the space of a gunshot, and the badge she now wore felt like a target over her heart.

But her father had taught her more than just how to shoot straight and read tracks. He'd taught her that justice wasn't about what was easy – it was about what was right.

And right now, what was right was finding the bastard who'd killed him.

A flash of memory hit her: Harris's last proposal, his cultured voice so certain of her eventual surrender. "Everything changes, Miss Wilson. The wise adapt. The foolish..." He'd gestured at the town, at her father's stubborn refusal to sell. "Well, they get left behind."

Grace checked her gun one last time and started following the tracks.

Time to see just how wise Mr. Harris was feeling now.

Chapter 2: The Stranger in Black

Grace's fingers traced the edge of her father's badge, now pinned to her own vest. Three days since the storm. Three days since she'd buried an empty coffin – the doctor's insistence on a closed casket still niggling at the back of her mind like a splinter she couldn't reach.

The office felt different in the pre-dawn quiet. Smaller. Or maybe she was just more aware of the shadows now, of all the places someone could hide with murder in mind.

Her father's desk drawer stuck slightly as she pulled it open. Thomas Wilson had been a methodical man – every warrant, every wanted poster filed with military precision. Which made the mess of papers stuffed in the back all the more suspicious.

Railroad contracts. Property deeds. Letters with fancy letterheads and carefully worded threats disguised as opportunities. And beneath them all, a half-finished letter in her father's familiar scrawl:

If you're reading this, Grace, I need you to understand—

The rest was blank.

A knock at the door sent her hand to her gun. Vincent Harris stood in the doorway, immaculate as always in a suit that probably cost more than her yearly salary. His smile didn't quite mask the calculation in his eyes.

"Miss Wilson. Or should I say, Sheriff Wilson now?"

"Deputy will do fine." She didn't stand. "What can I do for you, Mr. Harris?"

He stepped inside, each movement deliberate as a chess piece advancing. "I came to offer my assistance. And my deepest sympathies, of course. Your father was a... principled man."

"He was shot in the back. Doesn't take principles to know what kind of man does that."

Harris's smile didn't waver. "Indeed. Which is why I've taken the liberty of requesting additional security from the railroad company. These are dangerous times, and a lady sheriff—"

"Deputy," she corrected again, standing slowly. "And I don't recall asking for the railroad's help."

"Sometimes help comes whether we ask for it or not." He placed a card on her desk. "Should you reconsider. Day or night, Miss Wilson. I'm at your disposal."

The way he said it made her skin crawl.

After he left, Grace tucked the mysterious papers into her vest and headed for Ellie's saloon. The morning crowd would be thin – perfect for questioning potential witnesses without an audience.

The Golden Horseshoe was quiet as a church on Saturday night. Ellie stood behind the bar, while Doctor Cooper sat nearby, their heads close together in conversation. They jumped apart when Grace entered, Cooper knocking over his coffee cup in the process.

"Subtle," Grace remarked dryly. "Don't let me interrupt the morning's entertainment."

Ellie's cheeks darkened, but her voice stayed steady. "What can I get you, Sheriff?"

"Information." Grace leaned against the bar. "Anyone strange come through during the storm? Before or after?"

"Define strange," a deep voice drawled from the shadows.

Grace spun, gun clearing leather before her mind registered the movement. The stranger sat in the corner, all in black except for a silver watch chain that caught the morning light. His face belonged on a Roman statue – all sharp angles and classical beauty marred only by a roguish scar through his left eyebrow. But it was his eyes that held her: amber-brown with gold flecks, watching her with amused interest.

"Interesting welcome wagon you've got here," he said, not moving despite the gun aimed at his chest. "Do all new arrivals get such personal attention?"

"Only the ones who skulk in shadows." Grace kept her gun steady even as her pulse jumped traitorously. "Name?"

"Nathaniel Blackwood." His smile had an edge sharp enough to cut. "But most folks call me Nate."

"Most folks aren't pointing a gun at you."

"The day's still young."

Behind her, something crashed. Grace glanced back to see Ellie frozen, a broken glass at her feet, staring at Nate like she'd seen a ghost. The doctor was already moving to help her, but Grace caught the tremor in Ellie's hands.

Interesting.

"What brings you to Shadow Creek, Mr. Blackwood?"

He shrugged, the movement liquid as smoke. "Would you believe I'm here for the climate?"

"No."

"Smart girl." He stood slowly, and Lord help her, but he was tall. The kind of tall that made her want to step back, or maybe forward. "How about we discuss it over breakfast? I'm told the cafe here makes excellent—"

Gunshots exploded from the street, shattering windows and sending splinters flying. Grace dropped instinctively, but not before she saw Nate moving with the practiced grace of a gunfighter, drawing twin Colts from shoulder holsters.

"Friends of yours?" she asked as bullets chewed the bar above them.

His laugh was dark as sin and twice as tempting. "Lady, my friends usually buy me dinner first."

Bullets sprayed across the bar, sending glass and whiskey raining down. The acrid smell of gunpowder mixed with the sweet sting of spilled bourbon.

"Four of them," Nate said casually, as if discussing the weather. "Two by the bank, two behind the water trough."

Grace risked a glance. "Five. There's one on the roof of the general store."

His eyebrows rose slightly. "Impressive."

"I'm full of surprises." She checked her ammunition. "Got a preference?"

"Ladies' choice."

"Such a gentleman." She rolled her eyes but couldn't quite suppress a smile. "I'll take the roof and the bank. Try to keep up."

They moved like they'd rehearsed it – Grace rolling left while Nate went right, their shots synchronized as a dance. The first outlaw dropped before he could shift his aim, Grace's bullet finding him with lethal precision. Nate's guns sang a deadly duet, forcing the water trough bandits to duck and scatter.

Grace caught a flash of movement – the rooftop shooter repositioning. Without thinking, she grabbed Nate's arm, pulling him behind a pillar just as bullets splintered the wood where he'd been standing.

Time seemed to slow. She was suddenly very aware of his body pressed against hers, the solid warmth of him, the faint scent of leather and gunsmoke. His heartbeat was steady under her palm, unlike her own traitorous pulse.

"See something you like, Sheriff?" His whisper brushed her ear.

"Trying to decide if you're worth saving." She pushed away, ignoring the heat in her cheeks. "Behind you!"

Nate spun, his gun barking twice. The outlaw who'd tried flanking them fell, his own shot going wide.

"That's three," he called.

"Four," Grace replied, dropping the roof shooter with a clean hit. "One left."

The last bandit broke cover, running for a horse tethered nearby. Grace lined up her shot, but Nate's hand on her wrist stopped her.

"Wait."

The runner mounted up but instead of fleeing, he turned the horse in a tight circle, facing the saloon. The morning sun caught his face clearly for the first time.

"Well, well," Nate murmured. "Isn't that interesting."

Grace recognized him too – one of Harris's railroad guards, though she'd bet her badge that information wouldn't make it into any official report.

"Let him go," Nate said as she raised her gun again. "Sometimes a running man is more valuable than a caught one."

"That your professional opinion, Mr. Blackwood?"

"Among other things." His smile held secrets like a deck held aces.

The street was eerily quiet in the aftermath. Doctor Cooper emerged from behind the bar where he'd been shielding Ellie, his hands already reaching for his medical bag.

"Anyone hit?"

"Just the furniture," Grace answered, surveying the damage. "And Ellie's whiskey stock."

"Tch. Such a waste of good bourbon." Ellie's voice was steady, but her eyes kept darting to Nate and away, like someone avoiding a bright light. "I don't suppose any of you gentlemen want to explain why my saloon just became a shooting gallery?"

"Coincidence," Nate offered.

"Bad luck," Grace suggested simultaneously.

"Bullshit," Ellie declared, but there was a hint of fondness in her exasperation. "James, help me check the back room? I need to inventory the damage."

The doctor followed her, and Grace didn't miss how his hand brushed Ellie's lower back, or how Ellie leaned slightly into the touch. Well. That was new.

"Quite a team we make, Sheriff." Nate holstered his guns with practiced grace.

"We're not a team." But even as she said it, Grace couldn't help remembering how smoothly they'd moved together, how perfectly their shots had complemented each other. How his body had felt against hers...

She shut that line of thinking down hard. "Want to tell me what just happened?"

"Would you believe me if I said they were just poor losers from a poker game?"

"No."

"Smart girl." He said it differently this time – softer, almost admiring. "Let's just say I'm looking into some business irregularities. The kind that tend to end with dead sheriffs and convenient dust storms."

Grace's hand tightened on her gun. "You saying you know something about my father's murder?"

"I'm saying..." He stepped closer, close enough that she had to tilt her head back to meet his eyes. "That this town has secrets worth killing for. And you're not the only one looking for answers."

Her breath caught. This close, she could see the gold flecks in his eyes, the way his scar whitened slightly when he smiled. Dangerous, every instinct screamed. And yet...

"Why should I trust you?"

"You shouldn't." His honesty was oddly refreshing. "But you might want to check your father's correspondence from last March. Particularly anything regarding land surveys near the old silver mine."

Before she could demand more details, he tipped his hat and headed for the door. "Good shooting, Sheriff. I look forward to our next dance."

Grace watched him go, mind racing. How did he know about the mine? About her father's letters? And why did she have the unsettling feeling that Nathaniel Blackwood was either going to help her solve her father's murder – or end up being the death of her himself?

That night, alone in her bed, she dreamed of amber eyes and gunsmoke, of strong hands and dangerous smiles. In her dreams, the shooting played out differently. In her dreams, when he pressed her against that pillar...

Grace woke with a start, heart pounding, sheets twisted around her legs. Outside, the moon painted Shadow Creek in silver and secrets, and somewhere in the darkness, a stranger in black carried answers she wasn't sure she was ready to hear.

Chapter 3: Whispers in the Dark

The moon hung low over Shadow Creek, painting silver ribbons across Grace's desk as she sorted through her father's papers. The night air carried the lingering heat of day, heavy with secrets and the distant howl of coyotes.

Sleep had become an elusive luxury since the shooting. Every time she closed her eyes, she saw either her father's body or a certain stranger's amber gaze. She wasn't sure which disturbed her more.

The letter from March lay open before her, innocent as a rattler in tall grass. Land surveys, mining claims, and references to meetings she'd never known about. But it was the code in the margins that caught her attention – small marks her father had made, too deliberate to be idle doodling.

"Working late, Sheriff?"

Grace's gun cleared leather before she recognized the voice. Nate lounged in the doorway like sin given form, moonlight catching the silver in his watch chain.

"Most folks knock, Mr. Blackwood."

"Most folks aren't as interesting to watch." He moved into the office with that liquid grace that made her pulse skip. "Found anything worth dying for in those papers?"

She narrowed her eyes. "You tell me. You're the one who pointed me to them."

"Guilty." He perched on the edge of her desk, close enough that she caught a whiff of leather and something spicier. "Though I have to admit, the view from the roof across the street wasn't nearly as compelling as this one."

"You were watching me?"

"Someone had to." His expression turned serious. "Especially after what happened to the last person who went through those files."

A chill ran down her spine despite the warm night. "Are you threatening me, Mr. Blackwood?"

"Warning you." He leaned closer, and for a heart-stopping moment, she thought he might kiss her. Instead, he reached past her to tap the coded margin notes. "Your father wasn't the only one looking into the railroad's business. Just the only one who got caught."

Before she could process that, boots scuffed outside. They moved in sync – Grace diving left as Nate rolled right, just as bullets shattered the window. Glass rained down like deadly stars.

"Friends of yours?" she asked, echoing their conversation from the saloon.

His laugh was rough velvet in the darkness. "I make it a point not to befriend people who shoot at me. Present company excepted."

"I haven't shot at you." She fired through the broken window, earning a yelp from the shadows. "Yet."

"The night's still young."

They worked their way to opposite sides of the window, trading cover fire with the unseen attackers. Grace caught movement on the roof across the street – a familiar silhouette that made her blood run cold.

"The roof," she hissed.

Nate nodded, already moving. "Cover me."

"What? No!" But he was already out the door, running full tilt toward the adjacent building.

A bullet grazed her arm as she provided covering fire, the pain sharp and immediate. She bit back a curse, keeping her gun trained on the shadows where their attackers hid.

Suddenly, the night exploded in chaos. Nate appeared on the roof like an avenging angel, his guns blazing in the moonlight. The shadowy figures scattered, leaving one crumpled form behind.

"Hold still," Nate murmured, his fingers gentle despite their calluses as he examined her arm. They'd retreated to the back office, where a single lamp cast intimate shadows across their faces.

"I've had worse paper cuts," Grace protested, but her breath hitched as his touch traced the edge of the wound.

"I'm sure you have." His smile held a warmth she hadn't seen before. "But I'd hate to see this pretty arm scarred because of stubborn pride."

"My arm's not pretty, it's useful." Still, she didn't pull away as he cleaned the graze with whiskey from her father's not-so-secret desk drawer. "The shooter on the roof—"

"Got away." His jaw tightened. "But not before dropping this."

He pulled a crumpled paper from his pocket. Railroad company letterhead, partially burned, but Grace could make out words like "opposition" and "permanent solutions."

"Charming friends you have, Mr. Blackwood."

"Not friends." He wrapped a clean bandage around her arm, his touch lingering longer than strictly necessary. "And I told you, call me Nate."

"Fine. Nate." His name felt dangerous in her mouth, like tasting forbidden fruit. "Want to tell me why you're really here?"

Their eyes met in the lamplight. For a moment, she thought he might actually tell her the truth. Then a noise from the street shattered the moment – the distinct sound of Ellie's back door opening.

They moved to the window together, Grace acutely aware of how his body shielded hers as they peered out. A cloaked figure slipped from the saloon's back entrance, followed by Ellie herself. The stranger pressed something into Ellie's hands before disappearing into the shadows.

"Interesting," Nate murmured, his breath warm against her ear.

"You know something."

"I know many things." His eyes glinted with mischief. "Most of them dangerous."

"Does one of those dangerous things explain why you were watching my office tonight?"

He stepped back, and Grace immediately missed his warmth. "Let's just say I'm not the only one interested in your father's investigation. But I might be the only one who wants you to survive finding the truth."

As if to punctuate his words, they heard footsteps approaching the office. Grace drew her gun, but Nate's hand covered hers.

"That'll be Harris," he said softly. "Right on schedule."

"How did you—"

"Time for me to disappear." He moved to the back door, then paused. "Check the mining claims again. Your father's codes – they're not random doodles. They're coordinates."

Before she could respond, he vanished into the darkness like a shadow made of smoke and secrets.

Moments later, Harris's cultured voice carried through the broken window. "Miss Wilson? I saw the light... Good Lord, what happened here?"

Grace quickly tucked the railroad letter into her boot. "Just some late-night target practice, Mr. Harris. Can't let my skills get rusty."

"At this hour?" He stepped through the door, immaculate despite the late hour. His eyes cataloged the broken glass, the bullet holes, her bandaged arm. "My dear, if you needed protection—"

"I need answers." She met his gaze steadily. "About the mining claims. About my father's investigation. About why armed men seem so interested in old papers."

Something flickered behind his carefully pleasant expression. "Dangerous questions, Miss Wilson. Especially at night. One might think you're becoming... paranoid."

"Paranoid is when you imagine threats, Mr. Harris. I just count bullet holes."

Later that night, unable to sleep, Grace found herself at Doctor Cooper's office, following a hunch. The light was on despite the late hour, and through the window, she caught a glimpse of him treating a patient – a man whose face she couldn't see, but whose shoulder bore a fresh bullet wound.

Ellie was there too, her expression tight with worry as she helped the doctor. The patient's face remained in shadow, but something about his posture seemed familiar...

Grace forced herself to walk away. Too many secrets, too many players in a game she was just beginning to understand.

In her dreams that night, Nate's hands weren't just treating her wound. They traced fire across her skin, his touch alternately gentle and demanding. Dream-Grace didn't care about his secrets or his past. Dream-Grace only cared about the way his lips felt against her neck, the solid warmth of his body pressing her against the office wall, the way he whispered her name like a prayer and a sin wrapped into one...

She woke gasping, sheets twisted around her legs, the ghost of his touch still burning on her skin. Outside, the first hints of dawn painted the sky the exact color of his eyes when he smiled.

Dangerous, she reminded herself. Everything about him screamed danger.

But as she dressed for another day of hunting truth in a town full of lies, Grace had to admit – danger had never looked quite so tempting.

Chapter 4: Dangerous Alliance

The morning stage wasn't due for another hour, but Grace had learned from her father that trouble kept its own schedule. She settled into her watching position on the rocks overlooking Devil's Pass, where the road narrowed between steep canyon walls.

Movement caught her eye – a rider on the ridge opposite. Even at this distance, she'd recognize that black-clad figure anywhere. Nate raised his hand in a lazy salute, and she could almost see his insufferable smirk.

"Checking up on me again?" she muttered, though he couldn't possibly hear.

A flutter of movement in her peripheral vision made her turn. Three Apache warriors sat motionless on their ponies at the canyon's edge, watching the road with unsettling intensity. They hadn't been there a moment ago.

The stage appeared around the bend, kicking up dust. Grace counted four passengers through the windows, plus the driver and shotgun guard. Everything looked normal, except...

The guard's posture was wrong. Too stiff. And the driver kept looking back, not at the road.

"Damn it." She whistled sharply – a signal she hoped Nate would understand.

The attack came as suddenly as a desert storm. Six riders burst from a hidden ravine, guns blazing. The stage's horses reared in panic as the false guard turned his shotgun on the driver.

Grace's first shot took the traitor guard clean off his perch. Her second caught a bandit's horse, sending both crashing into the dust. Across the canyon, Nate's rifle cracked with deadly precision.

"Show-off," she muttered as he picked off another rider.

The stage was out of control now, horses panicking as the driver slumped over the reins. Grace swung onto her horse, spurring it down the rocky slope. She caught up to the stage just as it careened toward the canyon wall.

"Oh, this is stupid," she had time to think before launching herself from saddle to stage. She landed hard on the roof, nearly sliding off before catching the edge.

"Next time," Nate's voice came from impossibly close, "maybe we discuss the plan first?"

He was suddenly beside her on the roof, having appeared like a ghost. Together they worked their way forward, bullets whizzing past as the remaining bandits gave chase.

"You got a better idea?" Grace grabbed for the reins through the driver's window.

"Several. None of them involve suicide by stagecoach."

Working together, they managed to slow the horses, but not before the stage clipped the canyon wall. The whole vehicle lurched sickeningly. Grace lost her grip, sliding toward the edge—

Strong hands caught her, pulling her back against a solid chest. For a heartbeat, time seemed to stop. She could feel Nate's heartbeat against her back, his breath on her neck.

"I've got you," he murmured, and something in his voice made her shiver despite the desert heat.

Reality crashed back with the sound of gunfire. The remaining bandits were closing in, dust clouds billowing behind their horses like angry spirits.

"The mine," Nate shouted over the wind. "We can lose them in the tunnels."

"The mine that's probably going to collapse any day now?" Grace fired back, hitting one of their pursuers. "Brilliant plan."

"You got a better one, Sheriff?"

"Stop calling me Sheriff!" But she was already turning the team toward the abandoned mine entrance, using skills her father had taught her years ago.

The stage crashed through the rotting barrier, wooden splinters flying like shrapnel. Darkness swallowed them whole, the sudden transition from bright desert sun to cave darkness momentarily blinding.

"Everyone out!" Grace commanded the passengers. "Stay low, head deeper in!"

The following minutes were chaos – gunshots echoing off stone walls, the crash of the stage as the horses finally broke free, cursing in at least three languages as passengers scrambled for safety.

Then silence, broken only by falling pebbles and harsh breathing.

"Well," Nate's voice came from the darkness, impossibly close to her ear. "This is cozy."

"Shut up and help me check these tunnels." But she didn't move away from his warmth. "The passengers—"

"Are safe. I heard them take the north tunnel. The real question is what was so important in this stage that someone was willing to kill for it?"

A match flared, illuminating his face in golden light. This close, she could see the tiny scar at the corner of his mouth, the way his eyes seemed to hold secrets like a well held water.

"The mail pouch," Grace realized. "It's still in the wreck."

They found it under the overturned stage, along with something else – a false bottom in the strongbox, containing documents with the railroad company's letterhead.

"Well, well," Nate murmured, scanning the papers. "Looks like Mr. Harris has been a very busy man."

Before Grace could read them, rocks clattered behind them. They spun in unison, guns drawn, only to find Sarah standing in a shaft of light from a ventilation hole, looking as startled as they were.

"Sarah? What are you—"

But her friend was already running, disappearing into the maze of tunnels like a ghost.

"That's not suspicious at all," Nate drawled.

More rocks fell, larger this time. The whole mine groaned like a waking giant.

"We need to move," Grace started, but the tunnel behind them collapsed with a thunderous roar, forcing them deeper into the mine.

They ended up pressed together in a narrow passage, the air thick with dust and unspoken tension. Grace could feel every inch where their bodies touched, could hear the steady beat of Nate's heart against her palm.

"Any more brilliant ideas?" she whispered.

"A few." His voice was rough velvet in the darkness. "None of them particularly appropriate for a lady sheriff."

"Deputy," she corrected automatically, but the word came out breathier than intended.

His chuckle rumbled through both their bodies. "My mistake."

The mine shifted again, pressing them even closer. Grace's free hand found itself splayed against his chest, feeling the solid muscle beneath his shirt. His breath caught, and suddenly the air between them felt charged with something more dangerous than collapsing tunnels.

"Grace," he murmured, and the way he said her name should be illegal in at least three territories.

She tilted her face up, not entirely sure if she was going to tell him to shut up or—

Light flooded the tunnel as rocks shifted above them, breaking the moment. They pulled apart like guilty teenagers, though Grace could still feel the ghost of his touch.

"There's another way out," Nate said, his voice carefully neutral. "Through the old silver seam. If you trust me."

"I don't." But she followed him anyway, wondering which was more dangerous – the unstable mine or the way her heart raced every time he looked at her.

They emerged into late afternoon sun to find Doctor Cooper and Ellie having what appeared to be a picnic near the mine entrance. Both looked suspiciously unsurprised to see them.

"Fancy meeting you here," Ellie said with far too much innocence.

"Just showing the Sheriff some local attractions," Nate replied smoothly.

"Deputy," Grace corrected for what felt like the hundredth time.

"Of course." His smile held promises that made her pulse skip. "My mistake."

That night, alone in his rented room, Nate cleaned his guns and tried not to think about how Grace had felt pressed against him in the darkness. About how her hair had smelled like desert flowers and gunsmoke. About how her breath had hitched when he'd said her name...

He forced his thoughts back to the mission, to the papers they'd recovered, to all the reasons he couldn't afford distractions. But in his dreams, the mine collapse played out differently. In his dreams, the light never came, and he discovered exactly how sweet Shadow Creek's new deputy tasted when she gasped his name...

Chapter 5: Dance with the Devil

Grace stared at her reflection in the mirror, barely recognizing the woman who stared back. Sarah had worked miracles with the emerald green silk – "It matches your eyes, dear" – though Grace suspected a dress wouldn't make her any better at playing politics.

"Stop fidgeting," Sarah scolded, adjusting the neckline. "You look beautiful."

"I look like I'm playing dress-up." Grace touched her mother's locket, the only familiar thing about her appearance. "This is ridiculous. I should be patrolling, not dancing with snakes."

"Sometimes the best way to catch a snake is to charm it first." Sarah's hands trembled slightly as she fixed a loose curl. "Trust me."

Grace caught her friend's reflection – the shadows under her eyes, the way she kept glancing at her reticule where a letter peeked out. "Sarah, if you're in some kind of trouble—"

"Ladies!" Ellie burst in, resplendent in burgundy silk. "The carriages are arriving. And my, my, don't you clean up nice, Sheriff."

"Deputy," Grace corrected automatically, but her protest was lost in the rustle of skirts and last-minute adjustments.

The town hall had been transformed. Crystal chandeliers (borrowed from God-knows-where) cast golden light over silk-draped walls. A string quartet (definitely not local) played while Shadow Creek's finest mingled with railroad executives in tailored suits.

Vincent Harris materialized at her elbow like a perfectly-tailored ghost. "Miss Wilson. You look absolutely enchanting."

"Mr. Harris." She accepted his offered arm with all the enthusiasm of accepting a rattlesnake. "Quite a show you've put on."

"Progress deserves celebration, my dear." His smile never reached his eyes. "I believe you owe me the first dance."

The music shifted to a waltz. Harris's hand settled at her waist like a brand as he led her onto the floor. They moved together with practiced grace – he'd insisted on teaching her during his courtship – but now each turn felt like a move in a deadly game.

"Your father would have loved to see this," Harris murmured. "The future, coming to Shadow Creek at last."

"My father was shot in the back." Grace kept her smile fixed. "Somehow I doubt that was part of your grand vision."

His step didn't falter, but something flickered in his grey eyes. "Terrible business. Though I hear you've found... interesting company in your investigation. Mr. Blackwood, is it?"

Before she could respond, a new figure cut in smoothly. "Mind if I cut in?"

Nate stood there in a black suit that fit him like sin itself, looking more dangerous in formal wear than he did with his guns drawn. Harris's fingers tightened briefly on her waist before social graces forced him to step back.

"Of course." His smile was razor-sharp. "Miss Wilson is quite popular tonight."

Nate's hand settled at her waist like it belonged there, the heat of his touch burning through silk and propriety. His other hand caught hers, fingers intertwining with an intimacy that made her breath catch.

"You clean up surprisingly well for an outlaw," Grace murmured as they moved across the floor.

"And you wear authority beautifully for a lady in silk." His eyes traced her face with dangerous appreciation. "Though I notice you're still armed."

"A girl needs her accessories."

"Hmm." He pulled her fractionally closer than strictly proper. "Derringer in your garter?"

"Wouldn't you like to know."

His soft laugh rumbled through both their bodies. "More than I should."

They moved together like they'd been dancing for years, reading each other's signals as naturally as they had during the shootout. Grace was acutely aware of every point of contact between them, of the way his thumb traced small circles on her hand.

"Harris is watching us," she whispered.

"Harris isn't the only one." Nate's eyes flicked to the shadows beyond the windows. "Your friend Sarah just slipped out the back with a letter. And there's an Apache warrior watching from the church roof."

"You noticed all that while dancing?"

"I notice everything about you." His voice dropped lower, intimate. "Like how your pulse jumps when I do this."

He pulled her infinitesimally closer, his hand sliding a fraction lower on her back. Grace's heart betrayed her, skipping exactly as he'd predicted.

"That's hardly proper, Mr. Blackwood."

"I've never much cared for proper." His eyes held hers, dark with promise. "Have you?"

Before she could answer, movement by the punch bowl caught her attention. Doctor Cooper was watching Ellie speak with a well-dressed stranger, his expression thunderous. Ellie touched the stranger's arm, laughing at something he'd said.

"Trouble in paradise?" Nate murmured, following her gaze.

"The doctor's not the only one watching. Harris's man by the door hasn't taken his eyes off them."

"Smart girl." He spun her toward the edge of the dance floor. "Keep watching. I need to step out for a moment. Try not to miss me too much."

"In your dreams, Blackwood."

His smile turned wicked. "Frequently."

He disappeared into the crowd like smoke, leaving Grace feeling oddly bereft. She made her way to the punch bowl, pretending not to notice Sarah's return through the back door, face pale and hands shaking.

The next hour passed in a blur of forced smiles and careful conversations. Harris gave his speech about progress and prosperity, while Grace watched shadows move beyond the windows. Something was coming. She could feel it in her bones.

She found herself in a dark corridor, seeking a moment's respite from the politics and pretense. Footsteps approached – too heavy to be Sarah, too measured to be Nate.

"Miss Wilson." Harris emerged from the shadows, cologne and brandy heavy on his breath. "Hiding from your own party?"

"Just getting some air." She took a step back, but the wall was already against her shoulders.

"You look so much like your mother tonight." His hand reached for her face. "She understood about progress. About necessary sacrifices."

"Don't." Grace's voice was steel. "Don't you dare talk about her."

Movement behind Harris – a familiar silhouette in black. But before Nate could intervene, a shot cracked through the night air. Harris jerked, red blossoming on his pristine white shirt.

Grace moved instinctively, tackling him as more shots sparked off the wall. They crashed through a side door into the garden, roses perfuming the night air with surreal sweetness.

"Stay down!" Nate's voice, followed by return fire.

She pulled her derringer from its hiding place (not her garter, despite Nate's assumptions), covering the garden while checking Harris's wound. Clean through the shoulder – painful but not fatal.

"You're full of surprises," Harris gasped, managing to sound admiring despite the pain.

"You have no idea." She ripped her silk skirt for bandages, trying to ignore how her hands shook. Not from fear – from rage. Someone had brought violence to her town. Again.

Nate appeared like a shadow given form, gun still drawn. "Shooter's gone. Headed east, but..."

"But we can't pursue without leaving Harris unprotected." Grace met his eyes in the moonlight. "Go. I've got this."

He hesitated, then moved suddenly, pulling her into the shadow of a rose trellis. His kiss was fierce and unexpected, tasting of danger and unspoken promises. Grace's hands fisted in his jacket, drawing him closer even as her mind screamed about duty and propriety.

A distant shot split them apart. Nate pressed his forehead to hers for a heartbeat. "Stay alive, Sheriff."

"Deputy," she corrected breathlessly.

His laugh was rich and dark as sin. Then he was gone, leaving only the ghost of his kiss and the thunder of her heart.

Later, after the doctor had treated Harris and the party had dissolved into shocked whispers and speculation, Grace lay in her bed, reliving that kiss. In her dreams, there were no shots to interrupt them. In her dreams, his hands did more than just pull her close, and the rose garden witnessed things that would make even Ellie blush.

She woke to dawn painting her ceiling gold, her body humming with remembered pleasure and imagined touch. Outside her window, a single red feather lay on the sill – an Apache warning or blessing, she wasn't sure which.

One thing was certain: Shadow Creek's ghosts weren't done dancing yet. And neither, she suspected, was Nathaniel Blackwood.

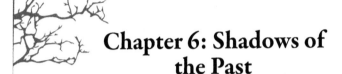

Chapter 6: Shadows of the Past

The bullet that had nearly killed Harris lay on Grace's desk like an accusation. She'd spent hours examining it, comparing it to the one she'd dug out of her father's office wall after his murder. The similarities were impossible to ignore.

"Same caliber," she muttered. "Same rifling marks. Same shooter."

"Or same gun," Nate's voice came from the doorway, making her start. He looked rough, like he hadn't slept. "Different shooters."

"Been investigating on your own, have you?" She kept her voice neutral, though last night's kiss still burned in her memory.

"That's what investigators do." He moved into the office with his usual liquid grace. "Found something you should see."

He placed a faded newspaper clipping on her desk. Grace's breath caught – her mother's obituary, dated twelve years ago. 'Tragic accident,' it claimed. But someone had underlined certain words, making connections she'd never seen before.

"Where did you get this?"

"Your mother's death wasn't an accident." Nate's voice was gentle, but his words hit like bullets. "The company was buying land even back then. She found something—"

"Stop." Grace stood so quickly her chair toppled. "You don't get to do this. You don't get to waltz in here with your secrets and your half-truths and dig up my past like it's some kind of—"

"Grace." He reached for her, but she stepped back.

37

"No. Who are you really, Nate? Because you're not just some drifter. You know too much. About the company, about my father's investigation, about..." Her voice cracked. "About my mother."

His expression shuttered. "Some questions are better left unanswered."

"That's not good enough anymore." She drew her gun, the action breaking her heart even as she did it. "Not after last night. Not after everything."

Something dangerous flickered in his eyes. "You going to shoot me, Sheriff?"

"If you don't start talking? Maybe."

The tension crackled between them like lightning before a storm. Then the church bells rang, breaking the moment. Through the window, Grace saw Father Michael hurrying across the street, looking over his shoulder like a man pursued.

"Think your priest knows something he shouldn't?" Nate asked, clearly glad for the distraction.

"Don't change the subject." But she was already moving to the window. "Although... he's been acting strange ever since Harris announced the new railroad route would cut through church property."

Before either could move, Sarah burst in, face flushed. "Grace, you need to come to the saloon. It's Ellie and the doctor—"

A gunshot punctuated her words. Grace and Nate shared a look, their personal conflict temporarily shelved.

"We're not done," she warned him.

His smile was sharp as a knife's edge. "Wouldn't dream of it, Sheriff."

They found chaos at the Golden Horseshoe. Doctor Cooper stood facing Ellie, his usually calm demeanor shattered. A smoking hole decorated the wall behind him.

"You knew?" The doctor's voice cracked. "All this time, you knew what they did?"

"James, please." Ellie's composure was cracking, tears in her eyes. "It's not what you think—"

"I treated their victims! Patched up their wounds while they—" He caught sight of Grace and Nate. "Ask her. Ask her about Chicago, about what she did for the railroad before she came here."

"That's enough." Nate's voice held a warning that made Grace look at him sharply. He knew something about Ellie's past.

"Is it?" Harris appeared in the doorway like a well-dressed demon. "I think we'd all like to hear about Chicago. About how certain people aren't who they claim to be." His eyes fixed on Nate. "Isn't that right, Marshal?"

The world tilted sideways. Grace's gun was in her hand before she registered drawing it. "Marshal?"

"Former marshal," Nate corrected quietly. "Until Chicago. Until I learned some truths about who I was really serving."

"And now you serve justice?" Harris's laugh was cruel. "Tell her about her father's letters. About how long you've really been watching Shadow Creek."

"Grace." Nate stepped toward her, but she backed away.

"Don't." The hurt in her voice surprised even her. "Just... don't."

She turned and ran, ignoring his call, ignoring everything except the need to get away. Her feet carried her to the church, where she found Father Michael in intense discussion with Sarah.

"—must tell her," Sarah was saying. "Before it's too late!"

They froze at Grace's appearance. Sarah's hand crushed a letter – the same type of paper as the threatening note Grace had seen earlier.

"Tell me what?"

But gunfire erupted before anyone could answer. Bullets shattered the stained glass, sending colored shards raining down like unholy rain. Grace tackled Sarah behind a pew as more shots peppered the church.

"Get to the vestry!" she shouted, returning fire through a broken window.

Movement caught her eye – figures in the bell tower. They hadn't been shooting at her, she realized. They'd been herding her.

The vestry door burst open. Nate stood there, guns drawn. "Move!"

"Why should I trust you?"

"Because I'm the only one here who's never lied to you." His eyes held hers. "I just didn't tell you everything."

More bullets splintered the pulpit. Grace swore under her breath and ran for the vestry, pulling Sarah with her. They emerged into the garden where Father Michael waited with surprising composure for a man under fire.

"The tunnels," he said, pulling aside a false panel in the garden wall. "Quickly."

The underground passage was narrow and dark. Grace found herself pressed against Nate as they moved, his body shielding her from unseen threats. Despite everything, her traitorous heart still raced at his proximity.

They emerged in the old silver mine – the same one from their earlier adventure. But this time, Nate pulled her into a hidden side tunnel before she could protest.

"Let me explain," he whispered, his breath warm against her ear.

"Now? Really?"

"Yes, now." His hands framed her face, and even in the darkness, she could feel the intensity of his gaze. "Because if those shots came from who I think they did, we might not get another chance."

"That's reassuring."

"Grace." The way he said her name still made her shiver. "I've been hunting the men who killed your mother for three years. Your father was helping me. That's why—"

Footsteps echoed through the mine. Grace pressed closer to Nate instinctively, feeling his heart race against her palms.

"Later," she whispered. "If we survive this, you'll tell me everything."

"Everything," he promised. Then, because he was Nate and timing had never been his strong suit, he kissed her.

It wasn't like their kiss in the garden. That had been fire and promise. This was desperation and need, apology and plea wrapped into one. Grace kissed him back with equal fervor, pouring all her confusion and hurt and want into it.

When they broke apart, she pressed her forehead to his chest. "I'm still mad at you."

"I know." She felt his smile against her hair. "You're beautiful when you're angry."

"Charmer." But she smiled despite herself. "Ready to shoot our way out of here?"

"With you? Always."

Later that night, alone in his room at the boarding house, Nate cleaned his guns and remembered. Remembered the first time he'd seen her, fierce and proud in her father's office. Remembered every smile, every sharp retort, every moment their bodies had drawn together like magnets finding true north.

In his dreams, the mine was darker, the danger more distant. In his dreams, they had time to explore every inch of tension between them, to map each other's bodies with hands and lips until the only secrets left were the sounds she made when he...

He woke with her name on his lips and determination in his heart. He'd tell her everything tomorrow. About Chicago, about her mother, about the real reason he'd come to Shadow Creek.

He just prayed she'd still look at him the same way after she knew the truth.

Chapter 7: Bloody Trails

Grace's fingers traced the worn edges of the floorboard beneath her father's desk. Something about its grain had caught her eye – too regular, too purposeful. Three taps revealed the hollow space beneath.

"Clever, Dad," she murmured, prying up the board. "Always did say the best safe was the one nobody knew to look for."

The hidden compartment yielded a leather portfolio, its contents protected from dust and time. Her hands trembled slightly as she opened it, revealing documents that made her breath catch. Railroad surveys, land deeds, and letters bearing signatures that made her eyes widen.

"Found something interesting?"

She didn't startle at Nate's voice anymore – she'd grown too accustomed to his habit of appearing like a shadow given form. He leaned in the doorway, looking unfairly handsome for someone who'd barely slept.

"Maybe." She met his eyes. "Feel like a ride? These mention a survey site up in Devil's Canyon."

His smile held equal parts warning and promise. "Alone in a canyon with an armed woman who's still mad at me? Sounds delightful."

"I'm not mad." She tucked the documents into her saddlebag. "I'm just keeping my options open about shooting you."

The ride to Devil's Canyon started quiet, the morning sun painting the desert in shades of gold and promise. Grace caught Nate watching her more than once, his expression unreadable.

"You're thinking too loud," she said finally.

"Just admiring the view." But his tone suggested he meant more than the landscape.

The canyon opened before them, its walls rising like ancient guardians. Grace checked her guns – a habit her father had drilled into her. Something felt wrong. The birds had gone quiet.

"Nate—"

The first shot kicked up dust at her horse's feet. The second would have taken her head off if Nate hadn't yanked her from the saddle.

They rolled behind a boulder as more bullets sparked off stone. Grace caught glimpses of figures on the canyon rim – at least six shooters, maybe more.

"Friends of yours?" she asked, returning fire.

"I make enemies more easily than friends." He fired twice, earning a cry from above. "Present company excepted."

"Flatterer."

They worked their way deeper into the canyon, using the rock formations for cover. Grace's mind raced – the ambush was too well-planned, too precise. Someone had known they were coming.

A bullet caught Nate high in the shoulder, spinning him against the rock wall. Blood bloomed across his black shirt like a deadly flower.

"Nate!" Grace's heart stopped, then restarted with painful force.

"Just a scratch," he grunted, but his face had gone pale beneath its tan.

More shots, closer now. They were being herded, Grace realized. And with Nate wounded...

"We need to split up." His voice was tight with pain. "I'll draw their fire—"

"If you think I'm leaving you, you've lost more blood than I thought." She ripped a strip from her shirt for a makeshift bandage. "Together, remember?"

Their escape was a blur of gunfire and desperation. Grace half-dragged, half-supported Nate through the canyon's twisting paths, his blood warm against her side. Each step seemed to cost him more effort, though he never stopped watching their back trail.

"Left," he muttered suddenly. "Hidden cave... behind the waterfall."

She would have missed it if he hadn't pointed it out – a narrow opening concealed by falling water and shadow. They stumbled inside just as fresh shots echoed through the canyon.

The cave was surprisingly deep, its walls smooth from ancient waters. Grace eased Nate down against the rock wall, trying to ignore how his breathing had grown labored.

"You know," he managed a weak smile, "when I imagined getting you alone in a dark cave, this wasn't quite what I had in mind."

"Shut up and let me look at that wound." But her hands were gentle as she peeled away his blood-soaked shirt.

The bullet had gone clean through his shoulder, but the bleeding wouldn't stop. Grace's hands shook as she used the remaining strips of her shirt for bandages.

"Like what you see?" His attempt at humor ended in a grimace.

"I've seen better." She hadn't – his chest was a roadmap of old scars and lean muscle that made her throat go dry despite the circumstances.

"Liar." His hand caught hers where it rested over his heart. "Your pulse is racing."

"That's the adrenaline."

"Is it?" His fingers traced patterns on her wrist. "Because mine's racing for an entirely different reason."

Heat bloomed in her cheeks. "You're delirious."

"Maybe." His other hand cupped her face, thumb brushing her bottom lip. "Or maybe nearly dying makes a man honest."

"Nate—"

"I love you." The words tumbled out like he couldn't hold them back. "Have since you pointed that gun at me in the saloon. Probably will till the day I die, which..." he coughed, "might be sooner than I'd like."

"Don't." Her voice cracked. "Don't you dare die on me, Nathaniel Blackwood. I haven't decided if I'm going to kiss you or kill you yet."

His laugh was weak but real. "Why not both?"

She kissed him then, tasting blood and desperation and truth. His hands tangled in her hair, pulling her closer despite his wound. They came together like a storm breaking, all the fear and want of the past weeks crystallizing into this moment.

"Grace," he breathed against her lips, then his body went slack.

"Nate?" Panic clawed at her throat. "Nate!"

His pulse was there, but weak. Too weak.

A shadow fell across the cave entrance. Grace spun, gun ready, but it was only Sarah, looking wild-eyed and desperate.

"Grace! Thank God. Doctor Cooper sent me – he's waiting at the old mission with supplies."

"How did you—"

"No time." Sarah's eyes darted to the canyon. "They're coming. There's a back way through the caves. I'll explain everything later, I promise."

Grace wanted to demand answers, but Nate's breathing was growing more labored. With Sarah's help, they half-carried him through twisting tunnels until they emerged near the abandoned mission.

Doctor Cooper waited with his medical bag, Ellie pacing nearby. Their own tensions seemed forgotten in the crisis.

"Get him inside," Cooper ordered. "Ellie, the laudanum."

What followed was a blur of blood and prayers. Grace held Nate down while Cooper dug out bullet fragments, her heart breaking at each pained sound he made. Ellie's hands were steady as she helped, though her eyes were haunted.

"He'll live," Cooper said finally. "But he needs rest. And watching. The fever might..."

"I'll stay with him," Grace said. It wasn't an offer.

Later, alone in the mission's small bedroom, Grace watched Nate's face in the lamplight. The fever made him restless, his mumbled words painting pictures of Chicago, of betrayal, of a love that terrified him more than bullets.

She dozed eventually, only to wake to his fingers tracing her face.

"You're still here," he murmured, voice rough but clear.

"Where else would I be?"

His smile was slow and warm. "Come here."

She moved closer, meaning only to check his fever. But his kiss was fire and healing and promise all at once. His hands pulled her onto the narrow bed beside him, need overwhelming caution.

"Your shoulder—"

"Will heal." His good hand tangled in her hair. "But if you don't kiss me again right now, I might actually die."

She laughed against his lips, relief making her giddy. "Drama queen."

But she kissed him anyway, and this time there was no interruption, no crisis, no reason to stop. Their bodies came together with the inevitability of lightning finding ground, each touch an exploration, each kiss a confession.

Dawn found them tangled together, her head on his good shoulder, his fingers tracing lazy patterns on her bare skin. Outside, a lone Apache warrior watched the mission before riding away with news that would change everything.

But that was tomorrow's problem. For now, there was just this – warmth and healing and a love that had bloomed in shadow but refused to die in the light.

Chapter 8: Betrayal and Loyalty

The mission's morning quiet was broken by the sound of breaking china. Grace rushed into the small kitchen to find Nate attempting to make coffee one-handed, shirtless and looking entirely too pleased with himself.

"You're supposed to be resting," she scolded, though her eyes lingered on the bandages crossing his chest.

"I'm supposed to be a lot of things." He pulled her close with his good arm. "Behaved isn't one of them."

"Clearly." But she melted into his kiss, savoring the simple intimacy of the moment.

A throat cleared from the doorway. Doctor Cooper stood there, medical bag in hand, looking distinctly uncomfortable.

"If you're well enough for that," he said dryly, "you're well enough for a proper examination."

Grace stepped back, cheeks warm. "I'll check the perimeter."

"You do that." Nate's wink promised later mischief. "Try not to miss me too much."

"I'll manage somehow."

Outside, the desert morning painted everything in shades of gold and promise. But something about Sarah's silhouette by the mission wall set Grace's instincts humming. Her friend was reading a letter, her hands shaking as she quickly tucked it away.

"Sarah?"

"Grace!" The smile was too bright, too quick. "I was just... checking on supplies."

Before Grace could press further, hoofbeats announced a rider. Vincent Harris approached like a dark prophet, his usual immaculate appearance somehow perfect despite the desert dust.

"Miss Wilson." His smile hadn't changed since the shooting. "A word, if you please? Privately."

Grace felt Nate's presence in the doorway behind her, tense as a drawn bowstring.

"Anything you need to say can be said here," she replied.

Harris's eyes flicked to Nate, then back to her. "Very well. I've come to offer you a chance to end this... unpleasantness. To secure your future and your father's legacy."

He dropped to one knee, producing a diamond ring that caught the morning light like frozen fire.

"Marry me, Grace. Let me protect you from what's coming."

The words hung in the air like gunsmoke. Behind her, she heard something that might have been Nate's knuckles cracking.

Grace stared at the ring, her mind racing. "That's quite an offer, Mr. Harris. Especially considering someone just tried to kill you at your own party."

"All the more reason to unite our interests." His smile turned predatory. "After all, we both want what's best for Shadow Creek."

"And what exactly is coming that I need protection from?"

Before Harris could answer, the mission door slammed. Nate had disappeared inside, his absence louder than any words.

"Think about it," Harris said, rising smoothly. "You have until sunset." He mounted up, then paused. "Oh, and Miss Wilson? Do give my regards to my brother when he arrives. He's most anxious to discuss certain... irregularities in the company books."

Grace found Nate in the small bedroom, methodically checking his guns despite his injured shoulder. The tension in his jaw could have cut steel.

"Going somewhere?" she asked.

"Figured you'd be busy planning a wedding." His voice was carefully neutral. "Congratulations, by the way. You'll make a lovely corporate wife."

"You're an idiot." She closed the door behind her. "A jealous, beautiful idiot."

He looked up sharply. "Grace—"

She crossed the room in three steps, straddling his lap before he could finish. His hands found her hips automatically, gun forgotten.

"I don't want his ring," she whispered against his mouth. "I don't want his protection. I want the truth. I want justice. I want..."

His kiss was fierce enough to steal her breath. They came together with desperate intensity, hands seeking skin, marking territory already claimed in the night.

"Say it again," he demanded between kisses.

"You're an idiot?"

"The other part."

A gunshot from the direction of town interrupted her reply. They broke apart, both reaching for weapons with practiced ease.

"Never a dull moment," Nate muttered, but his eyes were brighter than they'd been since Harris's arrival.

They found chaos at the Golden Horseshoe. The saloon's windows were shattered, and a well-dressed stranger who could only be Harris's brother stood in the street, facing down Doctor Cooper.

"You knew?" The doctor's voice cracked with betrayal. "All this time, you knew what they did in Chicago?"

Ellie stood between them, her usual composure cracking. "James, please. Let me explain—"

"Explain what? How you watched them destroy lives? How you helped cover it up?"

"I was undercover, you fool!" The words burst from Ellie like she couldn't hold them back. Then her hand flew to her mouth, horror dawning in her eyes.

Sarah chose that moment to appear, clutching a stack of papers. She froze at the tableau, then turned to run – straight into Grace.

Papers scattered like autumn leaves. Grace caught glimpses of railroad letterhead, coded messages, and a familiar signature that made her blood run cold.

"Sarah?"

"I'm sorry," her friend whispered. "They have my brother. I didn't have a choice."

More shots rang out, sending everyone diving for cover. Grace found herself behind the bar with Nate, while Harris's brother ducked into the storeroom with Ellie.

"Well," Nate said conversationally as bullets shattered bottles above them, "at least nobody's talking about that proposal anymore."

Grace couldn't help but laugh, though it held a hysterical edge. "You're still jealous."

"Terribly." He squeezed her hand. "Probably because I'm in love with you."

She turned to stare at him. "You choose now to say that?"

"Seemed as good a time as any." He grinned, that wild, beautiful smile that had first captured her heart. "Besides, I might get shot again before I get another chance."

"You're impossible." But she was smiling too.

"That's not a no."

Another volley of shots interrupted them. They moved in perfect sync, returning fire while working their way toward the storeroom.

Later that night, after the shooters had been driven off and the wounded tended to, Grace found Nate on the saloon's balcony. The desert stars painted silver patterns across his skin as he pulled her close.

"I meant it, you know." His voice was soft in the darkness. "Every word."

She traced the scar through his eyebrow, remembering their first meeting, their first kiss, every moment that had led to this.

"I know." She smiled against his lips. "I love you too, you impossible man."

Their kiss tasted of whiskey and gunsmoke and promises. Behind them, Sarah slipped away into the night with a letter that would change everything, while Harris's brother whispered secrets to Ellie that made her face go pale.

But those were tomorrow's battles. Tonight belonged to them, to hands rediscovering familiar territory, to kisses that held both apology and claim, to love forged in gunfire and sealed in starlight.

Dawn would bring new dangers, new betrayals, new truths. But for now, there was just this – two hearts beating in sync, two souls finding harbor in each other's arms, and a future worth fighting for.

Chapter 9: Storm Over Canyon

The town meeting wasn't Grace's idea. Harris had called it, ostensibly to discuss the railroad's progress, but his smile held secrets like a snake held venom.

"And now," Harris's voice carried through the packed town hall, "we should address the matter of certain... irregularities in our communications."

Grace felt Nate tense beside her as Sarah was called forward. Her friend looked small against the backdrop of angry faces, her usual composure cracking.

"Miss Anderson," Harris continued, "would you care to explain these?"

He held up letters – dozens of them. Each bore the railroad company's letterhead and Sarah's delicate handwriting.

"I..." Sarah's voice faltered.

"Perhaps I can help." Harris's smile widened. "These detail every shipment, every meeting, every move our dear deputy and her... companion have made in the past months."

The crowd's murmur turned ugly. Grace stepped forward, but Nate's hand on her arm stopped her.

"Wait," he whispered. "Something's wrong."

Thunder rolled outside, perfectly timed with Harris's next words. "Miss Anderson has been keeping us informed of certain... investigative activities."

"That's not all she's been doing." Doctor Cooper emerged from the crowd, holding a leather portfolio. "These were in my office. Records of payments, coded messages—"

A flash of lightning illuminated Sarah's face – not guilt, but fear. Her eyes darted to the window where, for just a moment, a shadow moved.

Then all hell broke loose.

The windows exploded inward as riders burst through them, guns blazing. The crowd scattered, screaming. Through the chaos, Grace saw Sarah being pulled onto a horse by unseen hands.

"Grace!" Nate's warning came just as more shots rang out.

They dove behind an overturned table as bullets splintered the wood around them. When they looked up, Sarah and her mysterious rescuers were gone.

"Church bells," Grace said suddenly, hearing the frantic pealing. "Someone's—"

"Hostages." Nate was already moving. "They're forcing people into the church."

The storm broke in earnest as they ran through the streets, rain turning dust to mud beneath their boots. Lightning revealed figures at the church doors, herding townspeople inside at gunpoint.

They found Ellie crouched behind a rain barrel, clutching a crumpled letter in her shaking hands.

"Three men inside," she whispered. "Plus whoever's in the bell tower."

"You should be taking cover," Grace said, but Ellie's laugh was bitter.

"After what I just received? I'd rather face bullets." She thrust the letter at Grace. "Chicago wasn't finished with me after all."

Before Grace could read it, gunfire from the tower forced them down. Nate returned fire, his aim deadly even in the storm.

"Back door," he said. "Through the cemetery."

"There is no back door," Grace started, but Ellie was already shaking her head.

"There's always a back door in a church, Deputy. Especially one built by men with secrets."

They circled around through the graveyard, rain washing the headstones clean of desert dust. Lightning revealed Harris's brother speaking intently with Doctor Cooper near the crypts, passing something between them.

Inside, they found chaos. The hostages were packed into the pews, while armed men patrolled the aisles. Grace caught glimpses of familiar faces – the baker, the blacksmith, children wide-eyed with terror.

A shot from Nate's gun shattered the lantern, plunging the church into darkness broken only by lightning flashes. They moved like shadows, taking down the gunmen with practiced efficiency.

But the last man had a surprise. He pulled a lever, and the altar slid sideways, revealing stone steps descending into darkness.

"Well," Nate drawled as the man disappeared below, "that's new."

"Stay with the townspeople," Grace ordered Ellie. "We'll—"

Thunder crashed directly overhead, and the church's ancient walls groaned. Debris started falling as the building shifted on its foundation.

"Everyone out!" Grace shouted. "Through the side doors!"

They helped evacuate the hostages, rain soaking them all to the skin. But when Grace turned back to the church, Nate caught her arm.

"The tunnel will collapse."

"There might be others down there!"

Their eyes met in a lightning flash, understanding passing between them. Together, then.

They descended into darkness just as part of the ceiling gave way behind them. The tunnel was older than the church, its walls lined with support beams that creaked ominously.

"You know," Nate said conversationally as they moved deeper, "this isn't how I planned to get you alone tonight."

"No? And how exactly did you plan it?"

His laugh echoed off the stone walls. "Involved a lot less mortal danger. A lot more—"

The tunnel collapsed behind them, the shock wave throwing them forward. They landed in a tangle of limbs, Nate's body cushioning her fall.

"You okay?" His hands moved over her, checking for injuries.

"Fine." But she didn't move away. In the darkness, every touch felt magnified, electric. "You?"

"Better than fine." His voice had dropped lower, intimate. "You're still on top of me."

Lightning from a shaft above illuminated them for a moment – his eyes dark with want, her hands splayed across his chest. The storm's energy seemed to crackle between them, turning fear to something headier.

His kiss tasted of rain and gunsmoke. They came together with desperate intensity, the danger outside making every touch more urgent, more real.

"Grace," he breathed against her neck. "My brave, beautiful Grace."

"Yours," she agreed, and felt his heart stutter beneath her palms.

Later – much later – they found their way to a cave opening in the canyon wall, the storm still raging outside. The tunnel's other secrets would have to wait.

That night, in her bed above the sheriff's office, Grace dreamed of stone passages and lightning-lit kisses. But in her dreams, they weren't running from danger. In her dreams, the cave became their sanctuary, where Nate laid her down on his coat and loved her with aching tenderness, whispering promises against her skin...

She woke to thunder and desire, the memory of his touch burning like brands on her flesh. Outside, Harris's brother crossed the street to the telegraph office, his face illuminated by lightning as he composed a message that would change everything.

And in her small room behind the saloon, Ellie stared at the letter from Chicago, tears mixing with the rain that leaked through her window.

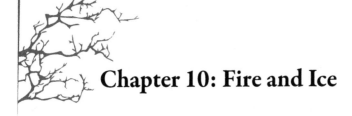

Chapter 10: Fire and Ice

The flames came alive at midnight, painting Shadow Creek's sky in shades of hell. Grace saw the glow from her office window seconds before the shouting started.

"Railroad office!" Someone was screaming. "Fire!"

She was running before the echo died, gun belt in one hand, badge catching firelight as she moved. The railroad company's pristine new building had become a torch against the desert night, flames licking up its walls like hungry demons.

"Water chain!" she shouted, organizing the townspeople who were already gathering. "Get those horses out of the stable!"

"Grace!" Nate appeared through the smoke like a ghost. "Harris is still inside!"

Of course he was. Because this night wasn't complicated enough.

They shared a look that contained an entire conversation, then plunged into the inferno together. The heat hit like a physical wall, smoke turning the elegant office into a maze of shadow and flame.

"Harris!" Grace's voice was lost in the roar of fire.

They found him in his private office, desperately stuffing papers into a strongbox.

"The building's collapsing," Nate shouted. "Leave it!"

"These documents are worth more than this whole town!" Harris's usual composure had cracked, revealing something darker beneath.

A burning beam crashed down, barely missing Grace. Nate pulled her back, his body shielding her from sparks.

"We don't have time for this." He drew his gun. "Either come with us now, or I'll carry you out unconscious."

Harris's laugh was edged with madness. "You always did favor the direct approach, didn't you? Even in Chicago."

The building groaned ominously. Grace grabbed the strongbox while Nate took Harris's arm in a grip that made the banker wince.

They barely made it out before the roof collapsed, emerging into clean air that felt like heaven after the smoke. Grace stumbled, and Nate caught her, pulling her close with desperate strength.

His kiss tasted of smoke and fear, public propriety forgotten in the wake of almost dying. Again.

"If you two are quite finished," Harris's dry voice interrupted, "I believe you have something of mine."

Grace held the strongbox against her chest like a shield. "Actually, Mr. Harris, I believe these are evidence now."

"Evidence?" His laugh held no humor. "Of what? Progress? Civilization? You're just like your father – too blind to see the future when it's staring you in the face."

"The future doesn't usually involve quite so many bodies," Nate's voice was steel wrapped in silk.

A shot cracked through the night. Grace felt the bullet pass close enough to stir her hair before Nate tackled her behind a water trough, the strongbox trapped between them.

"You know," she muttered as more shots peppered their cover, "we really need to stop meeting like this."

"What, you don't enjoy our romantic evenings?" His grin was wild in the firelight.

Harris had disappeared in the confusion, but Grace caught glimpses of movement on the rooftops – multiple shooters, well-positioned. This was no opportunistic attack.

"Grace!" Sarah's voice, impossibly, from the shadows of the alley. "This way!"

"It could be a trap," Nate warned, but Grace was already moving. Sometimes you had to trust your heart over your head.

They found Sarah in the stables, her face streaked with soot and something that might have been tears. "There's something you need to see. Both of you."

But before she could explain, three Apache warriors materialized from the darkness. The eldest spoke in rapid-fire language that Grace couldn't follow, but Nate's face went grave.

"We need to move," he said. "Now."

They escaped through the back alleys, the strongbox heavy with secrets. Behind them, the railroad office collapsed in a shower of sparks that lit the sky like fallen stars.

Grace found herself in Nate's room at the boarding house, spreading the saved documents across his bed while he cleaned smoke residue from his guns.

"I knew Harris in Chicago," he said suddenly, his voice quiet. "I was a Federal Marshal, investigating corporate corruption. Harris was... He was supposed to be our inside man."

"What happened?"

"What always happens." His bitter laugh held years of pain. "Money talked louder than justice. By the time I realized he'd turned, it was too late. Good men died. I barely got out alive."

Grace crossed to him, taking the gun from his hands. "Is that why you came here? Hunting him?"

"I came here hunting justice." His hands framed her face. "I stayed because of you."

Their kiss tasted of smoke and truth and promises. They came together with the desperate need of people who'd seen death too close, hands seeking skin, mouths trading secrets without words.

Later, much later, they lay tangled in his sheets while desert stars painted silver patterns through the window. The strongbox's contents lay forgotten, overshadowed by the way he whispered "I love you" against her skin, by the stories his scars told under her fingers.

A knock interrupted their peace. Ellie stood there, looking both apologetic and determined. "Doctor Cooper proposed."

"Congratulations?" Grace sat up, clutching the sheet.

"We're eloping. Tonight. Need witnesses." Ellie's eyes held a plea. "Before... before things get worse."

"Things?" Nate was already reaching for his guns.

"The Indians' warning." Ellie's voice shook. "Storm's coming, they said. But not the kind that brings rain."

Dawn found them in the small chapel outside town, watching Ellie and Cooper exchange vows while first light painted the desert gold. Grace leaned against Nate, his arm warm around her waist, remembering their own first kiss in another church so recently.

But the peace couldn't last. Sarah waited outside with news that made Ellie's face go pale, while in the distance, dust clouds promised riders approaching.

The storm was coming, just as the Indians had warned. But for now, there was this moment – love claimed in firelight, truth offered in darkness, and hope blooming like desert flowers after rain.

Chapter 11: Dance with Shadows

The railroad company's masquerade ball transformed the newly rebuilt office into a fever dream of silk and secrets. Crystal chandeliers cast fractured light across masked faces, turning familiar townspeople into elegant strangers.

Grace adjusted her emerald mask, feeling oddly vulnerable despite the gun hidden in her gown's clever folds. Sarah had outdone herself with the dress – black silk that shimmered green in certain lights, like a raven's wing in sunshine.

"My dear Deputy," Harris appeared beside her, resplendent in a golden Venetian mask. "Or should I say, midnight goddess?"

"Mr. Harris." She accepted his offered champagne without drinking it. "Quite a resurrection for a building that was ashes last week."

"Phoenix-like, wouldn't you say?" His smile held secrets. "Speaking of resurrections, I had the most interesting conversation about your father recently..."

Grace's heart stuttered, but before Harris could continue, a figure in black cut between them. Nate's wolf mask couldn't hide his identity – not from her, not when she knew every line of his body by heart.

"I believe this dance is mine," he said, sweeping her away from Harris's knowing smile.

They moved together like smoke, like shadow, like two parts of the same dangerous whole. His hand at her waist burned through silk and propriety.

"You clean up nicely, Mr. Blackwood."

"And you," his voice dropped lower, intimate, "are trying to kill me with that dress."

"You should see what's beneath it," Grace whispered, delighting in how his steps faltered.

"Tease." His hand tightened at her waist. "But I have to step out for a moment. Watch Harris's brother – he's been too interested in the garden entrance."

He disappeared into the crowd like a shadow melting into darkness. Grace caught glimpses of another masked figure following him – someone whose bearing screamed 'law enforcement' to her trained eye.

Across the room, Ellie and Doctor Cooper were arguing in fierce whispers, their own masks slightly askew. The doctor stormed off, leaving Ellie staring at a piece of paper in her trembling hands.

"Trouble in paradise?" Harris's brother appeared at Grace's elbow, his silver mask catching candlelight. "Such a shame about their wedding plans."

"How did you—"

"I make it my business to know things, Deputy Wilson." He sipped his champagne. "For instance, I know about a certain letter your father wrote, just days before his... unfortunate accident."

Grace's heart stopped, then raced. "My father's dead."

"Are you sure?" His smile was pure Harris – all teeth and hidden knives. "Because I could swear I saw his handwriting on a very recent document."

Movement by the garden doors caught her attention – Sarah, slipping outside with a familiar leather portfolio. The same one she'd seen in Harris's office during the fire.

"Excuse me," Grace murmured, already moving.

The conservatory was a crystal palace of exotic plants, steam from the heating system creating a tropical atmosphere that made her dress cling. She followed Sarah's trail past palm fronds and blooming orchids.

A hand grabbed her from behind, pressing a sweetly-scented cloth to her face. Grace fought, but the world was already going dark at the edges.

"Sorry about this," Sarah's voice seemed to come from far away. "But we need to know what you know."

Grace's last conscious thought was of Nate's voice, shouting her name.

She woke to gunfire and breaking glass. Strong arms carried her, and for a moment she fought until she recognized Nate's scent, his touch.

"Easy, love." His voice was tight with controlled rage. "I've got you."

They were in a hidden alcove of the conservatory. Through the fogged glass, she could see masked figures exchanging fire among the plants.

"Sarah?" Her voice was rough.

"Got away." Nate checked her for injuries with gentle hands. "Along with her... associates."

"She said 'we.'" Grace's mind was clearing. "And Harris's brother, he said something about my father—"

Nate silenced her with a kiss that tasted of desperation and gunpowder. She melted into him, their masks tangling as the kiss deepened into something wild and needed.

"Thought I'd lost you," he breathed against her mouth.

"Never." She pulled him closer, desire cutting through the last of the drug's fog. "Take me home."

They barely made it to his room. Masks and fancy clothes created a trail to his bed, where they came together with the desperate intensity of people who'd seen death too close. Every touch was a promise, every kiss a confession of things too deep for words.

Later, watching desert stars through his window, Grace told him about Harris's brother's hints.

"Could it be true?" She traced patterns on his chest. "Could my father be alive?"

"I don't know." He kissed her temple. "But we'll find out. Together."

That night, Nate dreamed of Grace in her masquerade gown, but in his dreams, they weren't interrupted. In his dreams, he slowly unveiled her like a precious gift, worshipping every inch of silk-clad skin until she begged for mercy he was disinclined to give...

He woke hard and aching, to find reality even better than fantasy – Grace warm and willing in his arms, her kisses chasing away the shadows of conspiracy and threat.

Outside, Sarah met with a hooded figure, passing notes that would change everything. And in his office, Harris's brother smiled at a telegram that confirmed his worst suspicions.

The masquerade was over, but the real dance of shadows was just beginning.

Chapter 12: Bloody Dawn

The gold shipment was due at dawn. Grace watched the sun paint the canyon walls blood-red, trying to ignore how the color felt like an omen.

"Penny for your thoughts?" Nate's voice was warm against her ear as he joined her on the ridge.

"They're worth at least a nickel." She leaned back against him, savoring his solid presence. "Something feels wrong."

"Besides the fact that Deputy Carter's been watching us through a spyglass for the last hour?"

Grace stiffened. Carter was her father's most trusted deputy, now hers. "You're sure?"

"As sure as I am that you're wearing that lace thing I like under your shirt."

She elbowed him, but couldn't help smiling. "Focus, Blackwood."

"I am focused." His hands settled on her hips. "Very, very focused."

The sound of approaching wagons interrupted what promised to be an interesting conversation. The gold shipment rounded the bend below – three heavily armed wagons carrying the railroad's payroll and, if their suspicions were correct, evidence of massive corruption.

"Here we go," Grace murmured, straightening her badge.

The first shot came from behind them.

Nate moved faster than thought, tackling her as bullets churned the dirt where she'd stood. They rolled behind a boulder, guns already drawn.

"Still think I'm paranoid about Carter?" Nate asked, returning fire.

"You're never going to let me live this down, are you?"

"Not a chance, love."

The canyon erupted in gunfire. Below, masked riders swarmed the wagons like locusts, while above, Carter's men had them pinned down.

"I count twelve," Nate said, dropping another attacker.

"Thirteen." Grace's shot knocked a rider from his horse. "You missed one behind the rocks."

"Show-off."

A familiar voice rang out from the wagons – Harris's brother, directing the raid with military precision. The gold wasn't their real target, Grace realized. They were after something else.

"The third wagon," Nate said, reading her mind. "They're focusing on it."

"Cover me."

"Grace—"

But she was already moving, using the chaos as cover. Nate's exasperated curse followed by precise covering fire made her smile despite the danger.

She reached the wagon just as Harris's brother found what he was looking for – a false bottom concealing documents. Their eyes met through his mask.

"You know," he said conversationally, "your father asked the same questions you are. Before he... disappeared."

"My father's dead."

"Is he?" He tossed her an envelope. "Because he has excellent penmanship for a corpse."

A shot cracked out. The man jerked, blood blooming on his shoulder, and Grace caught a glimpse of Ellie in the rocks, holding a rifle with surprising expertise.

"Federal Marshal!" Ellie's voice carried authority Grace had never heard before. "Drop your weapons!"

The battle shifted instantly. Carter and his men turned on the robbers, revealing themselves as part of the conspiracy. Grace found herself caught in the crossfire, the letter burning in her pocket.

"Grace!" Nate's warning came just as a bullet creased his arm. He stumbled, exposed.

Time slowed. She saw Carter taking aim at Nate, saw the glint of sunlight on his gun barrel. Her shot took Carter in the shoulder before he could pull the trigger.

When the dust settled, most of the robbers had escaped, taking the mysterious documents with them. But they had prisoners – including Carter, who wasn't talking, and the wounded brother of Harris, who talked too much without saying anything.

"Federal Marshal?" Grace asked Ellie later, as Doctor Cooper tended Nate's wound.

"Former." Ellie's smile was sad. "Like your man there. Chicago changed a lot of us."

"Speaking of change," Doctor Cooper said, examining old medical records, "these autopsy reports from your father's death... there are inconsistencies."

Before he could elaborate, an Apache rider appeared like a ghost at the office door. He spoke rapidly to Nate, then disappeared as suddenly as he'd arrived.

"What did he say?" Grace asked, noting how Nate's face had gone grim.

"They're leaving. All of them. Something's coming that even they won't face."

That night, knowing tomorrow would bring more danger, Grace and Nate made camp under the stars. The bottle of wine and basket of food Sarah had packed seemed incongruous with their battered state, but somehow perfect.

"Read it," Nate said quietly, nodding to the letter she'd been avoiding.

Grace's hands shook as she opened the envelope. The handwriting was achingly familiar. Her father's words jumped out at her, but before she could read further, Nate tensed.

"Company," he whispered.

They rolled apart just as shots shattered their wine bottle. Grace caught a glimpse of Carter's badge glinting in the moonlight – he'd escaped custody.

"You know," Nate said as they returned fire, "most couples just have dinner on date night."

"Where's the fun in that?" She grinned, the letter safely tucked away for later.

Later, much later, they lay tangled together in his bed, the letter temporarily forgotten in the wake of nearly losing each other again.

"I should go," Grace murmured against his chest, making no move to leave.

"You should stay." His arms tightened around her. "Forever."

The word hung between them, heavy with promise. Grace lifted her head to meet his eyes, finding everything she needed to know there.

"Forever's a long time, Blackwood."

His smile was slow and sweet. "Not long enough, love. Not nearly long enough."

Outside, Ellie met secretly with her federal contacts, while Sarah watched from shadows, playing her own dangerous game. And somewhere in the darkness, a man with familiar handwriting planned his next move.

But for now, there was just this – two hearts beating in sync, two souls finding harbor in each other, and a love strong enough to weather whatever storm was coming.

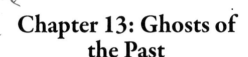

Chapter 13: Ghosts of the Past

Grace found the diary while cleaning out her father's old chest – a small leather-bound book with her mother's flowing script. The pages smelled of lavender and secrets.

"I remember her writing in this," she told Nate, who was cleaning his guns at her desk. "Every night, like clockwork."

"You never mentioned your mother much."

"Neither did Dad, after..." She opened the diary, then froze. Pressed between the pages was a telegram about the railroad, dated weeks before her mother's death.

Nate's hands stilled on his gun. "Grace—"

"She knew something." Grace's voice shook. "She was investigating them, wasn't she? Like Dad. Like..."

"Like me." He set the gun down carefully. "It's time you knew the truth."

She looked up, caught by something in his tone. "Nate?"

"I wasn't just any Federal Marshal." He crossed to her, touched her face with callused fingers. "I was assigned to your mother's case. After she died, your father contacted me. We've been building this case for years."

The world tilted sideways. "Years? You knew my father?"

"Grace—"

A knock interrupted them. Harris stood in the doorway, immaculate as always.

"Sorry to interrupt this touching moment," his smile was pure venom, "but we need to discuss your future in this town, Miss Wilson. Or rather, the lack of it."

"Your timing's impeccable as always, Harris." Nate's hand stayed on his gun. "Like a vulture sensing death."

"Charming analogy." Harris stepped into the office. "Though perhaps not entirely inappropriate. Doctor Cooper just had an unfortunate accident."

Grace was moving before he finished speaking. "What did you do?"

"Me? Nothing." His innocence was as false as his smile. "Though mixing up medicine bottles can be so tragically easy..."

They found chaos at the doctor's office. Cooper lay convulsing on the floor while Ellie frantically searched through broken bottles.

"Someone switched his medicines," she said, tears streaming. "All of them are mislabeled."

Grace's law enforcement training kicked in. "Which one did he take?"

"His usual headache powder, but—" Ellie stopped, revelation dawning. "The cellar. He keeps backup supplies in the cellar!"

The cellar door was locked, but Nate's boot made short work of it. What they found inside stopped them cold – not just medical supplies, but weapons. Crates of them.

"Well," Nate drawled, "that's not standard medical equipment."

"Focus," Grace snapped, grabbing the correct medicine. They managed to save Cooper, but it was close. Too close.

"The weapons cache," Grace said later, alone with Nate in her office. "You knew about it."

"Yes." He didn't insult her by denying it.

"How long?" When he hesitated, she pressed. "How long have you been playing me, Nate?"

"Playing you?" His laugh was bitter. "Grace, everything I've done has been to protect you. Your father asked me to watch over you before he—"

"Before he what?" She seized on the slip. "You know where he is, don't you?"

"Grace—"

"Don't." She backed away from his reach. "Just... don't."

Looking at him hurt, like staring at the sun. All this time, he'd known. Every kiss, every touch, every whispered promise – how much had been real, and how much had been his mission?

"I never lied about loving you." He stayed where he was, letting her have space. "That's the one true thing in all this mess. I came here for justice, but I stayed for you."

"Prove it." Her voice cracked. "Tell me everything."

"I can't." The pain in his eyes matched hers. "Not yet. But I can show you something."

He laid his Marshal's badge on her desk. "I'm done with secrets. Whatever comes next, I choose you. Over justice, over duty, over everything."

"Everything?" She was moving toward him despite herself, drawn like iron to lodestone.

"Everything." His hands shook as they framed her face. "I love you, Grace Wilson. The rest is just details."

Their kiss tasted of truth and tears and promises. They came together like storms meeting, all the fear and anger transmuting into desperate need. Clothes marked trails to her desk, where he loved her with fierce tenderness, whispering declarations against her skin.

Later, watching the desert sunset paint her office gold, Grace remembered their first meeting – how he'd sat in Ellie's saloon like sin given form, how she'd known even then that he would change everything.

"Penny for your thoughts?" His voice was warm against her neck.

"Just remembering the first time I wanted to shoot you."

"Which time was that?"

"All of them." But she smiled as she said it.

A knock interrupted their peace. Sarah stood there, pale but determined, holding papers that made Nate curse softly.

"You need to see these," she said. "And... Ellie's gone. Left a note about 'finishing what we started in Chicago.'"

The papers would change everything. But for now, Grace held onto this moment – the weight of truth between them, the strength of love tested by fire, and the promise of a future worth fighting for.

Even if they had to burn down the whole world to claim it.

Chapter 14: Cards Revealed

The man waiting in Ellie's empty saloon wore Grace's father's face like a mask that didn't quite fit. Thomas Wilson had aged decades in months, but his eyes – her eyes – were exactly as she remembered.

"Hello, sweetheart."

Two words. Just two words to shatter her world.

"You're dead." Her voice sounded distant to her own ears. "I found you. I held you while you—"

"While I what?" His smile was gentle, familiar, wrong. "While I bled? Did you check the pulse, Grace? Did you look under the bandages?"

Her gun was in her hand without conscious thought. "Stop talking."

"Your mother taught you better gun control than that." He nodded at her trembling hands. "Remember? 'Steady hands, steady heart.'"

"Don't." The word was a bullet. "Don't you dare talk about her."

"I did it to protect you." He took a step forward. "Both times. Your mother's death, my... disappearance. All of it was to keep you safe."

"Safe?" She laughed, the sound raw as a wounded animal. "I buried you. I mourned you. I—"

"Put the gun down, Grace." Nate's voice, warm and sure behind her. "Let him explain."

"You knew." She didn't turn. "All this time..."

"Not all of it." Nate moved beside her, close enough to touch but respecting her space. "Just the last month. Since the mine."

"The mine." Grace's laugh held no humor. "Of course. When I was too busy almost dying to notice whatever game you two were playing."

"It wasn't a game." Her father's voice cracked. "Harris has plans for this town that go beyond mere railroad expansion. The mine's silver deposits are just the beginning."

"The railroad's bringing progress," she quoted Harris's words mockingly. "Civilization."

"The railroad's bringing an army." Nate moved to the window, scanning the street. "Private security forces, weapons stockpiles, enough manpower to control the entire territory."

"And you couldn't tell me this because...?"

"Because Harris has something on everyone," her father said. "Everyone except you. Your clean reputation was our only advantage."

Before Grace could respond, the saloon's back door burst open. Doctor Cooper stumbled in, supporting a bleeding Ellie.

"They found our witness," Ellie gasped. "Sarah... she..."

"Where?" Grace was already moving.

"The church." Cooper's hands were red with someone else's blood. "She said to tell you 'the records are safe.'"

They found Sarah in the church courtyard, papers scattered around her like fallen leaves. She was alive, barely, clutching a leather portfolio to her chest.

"Had to..." she whispered as Grace knelt beside her. "Had to make them think they got everything..."

"Save your strength." Grace turned to Cooper. "Can you—"

"Already working on it." The doctor's hands were sure despite the circumstances.

Hoofbeats approached – Harris and his men, riding like demons in the gathering dusk.

"Time to choose sides," Harris called out to the gathering crowd. "Progress or obsolescence. Future or past."

The town divided like the Red Sea, neighbors facing neighbors across an invisible line. Grace stood with her father and Nate, watching former friends cross to Harris's side.

"Last chance, Miss Wilson." Harris's smile was colder than desert nights. "Join the future."

"I choose justice." She raised her father's badge. "I choose truth."

"You choose death." He raised his hand to signal his men.

An arrow thudded into the ground between them. On the church roof, Apache warriors materialized like spirits, bows drawn.

"Not today," Nate's voice held steel and satisfaction.

Later, in the safety of night, Grace let herself break. Nate held her as she raged and wept, his hands gentle in her hair.

"I thought I was alone," she whispered against his chest. "All this time..."

"Never." His kiss tasted of promises. "Never alone again."

They came together with desperate tenderness, reaffirming life in the face of death's shadow. Every touch was a promise, every kiss a declaration of things too deep for words.

"Marry me," he whispered against her skin.

She raised her head, surprised. "Now? With everything—"

"Now. Tomorrow. Always." His smile was fierce and beautiful. "I want forever, Grace Wilson. However long or short that might be."

"Yes." She kissed the surprise off his face. "Yes to forever."

Dawn found them tangled together, planning futures that might never come. Outside, the town held its breath as storm clouds gathered. Sarah recovered in the doctor's care while Ellie and Cooper exchanged vows in secret, witnessed by Grace's father and an Apache chief who smiled like he knew something they didn't.

The war wasn't over. Harris's plans still threatened everything they loved. But for now, there was this – love stronger than betrayal, truth worth dying for, and a future worth fighting for.

Even if they had to rebuild the whole world to claim it.

Chapter 15: Before the Storm

Desert sunsets had always been beautiful to Grace, but this one felt different – like the sky was bleeding out over Shadow Creek. Tomorrow would change everything, one way or another.

"Penny for your thoughts?" Nate's arms slipped around her waist as she watched from the sheriff's office window.

"Just wondering how many more sunsets we'll see." She leaned back against him. "That's terribly dramatic of me, isn't it?"

"Absolutely shameful." His kiss brushed her temple. "I expect at least fifty years of sunsets with you, Mrs. Almost-Blackwood."

The makeshift war council gathered in Ellie's saloon – her father, the Apache chief Running Fox, and a dozen trusted townspeople. Maps covered the bar where bottles usually stood.

"Harris's men are here and here," Thomas Wilson pointed to the canyon approaches. "But his main force..."

"Is coming by train." Ellie's entrance silenced the room. She dropped a telegraph on the map. "Special delivery from my colleagues in the Federal Marshal's office."

"Colleagues?" Grace raised an eyebrow.

"Surprise." Ellie's smile was sharp as a knife. "Turns out I'm not just a pretty face serving whiskey."

Before Grace could probe further about Ellie's revelation, Harris's brother burst through the door, his usually immaculate appearance disheveled.

"They're coming." He dropped a stack of papers on the bar. "Earlier than we thought. Vincent's lost whatever sanity he had left."

"And we should trust you because..." Grace let the question hang.

"Because I just burned every bridge I had to bring you these." He spread out documents bearing the railroad's letterhead. "Including proof about your mother's death."

Doctor Cooper appeared at Grace's elbow, medical files in hand. "These match the irregularities I found. The timing, the unusual marks—"

A commotion outside interrupted them. Running Fox's scouts had returned, their expressions grave as they reported in their native tongue.

"They say the spirits are leaving the valley," Nate translated. "Even the animals are fleeing."

"Dramatic bunch, aren't they?" But Grace noticed how her father's hand tightened on his gun.

The evacuation began at dusk. Women, children, and those unwilling to fight streamed out of town in wagons protected by Apache warriors. Each departure felt like another piece of Grace's heart being carved away.

"Someone's watching from the church tower," Nate murmured, his hand warm on her lower back.

"I know." She'd felt those eyes too. "One of ours?"

"That's what worries me."

Later, as stars began painting the sky silver, they found a moment alone in their room above the sheriff's office. Grace traced the familiar scars on Nate's chest, memorizing him by touch.

"Having second thoughts about marrying an outlaw?" His voice was light, but his eyes were serious.

"Former outlaw." She kissed a scar near his heart. "Former marshal. Former lot of things. But always mine."

"Always yours." He pulled her closer, his kiss tasting of promises and gunpowder. "Though I was hoping for a proper wedding. White dress, church bells, your father not cleaning his gun in the front row..."

"Since when do we do anything properly?" But she smiled against his mouth.

They came together with desperate tenderness, knowing each touch might be their last. Clothes marked a trail to their bed, where they loved each other with the fierce intensity of people stealing time from fate.

"I have something for you," Nate said later, producing a simple gold ring. "It was my mother's."

Grace's throat tightened as he slipped it on her finger. "It's perfect."

"Like you."

"Now who's being dramatic?"

Their laughter faded as running footsteps approached. A knock interrupted their peace – Thomas Wilson, looking grim.

"Grace." His voice cracked. "There's something you need to know about tomorrow. About why I really came back."

But before he could continue, gunfire erupted in the street. They rushed to the window to see the church tower ablaze, signals flashing from its heights.

"Looks like tomorrow came early," Nate growled, reaching for his guns.

Grace caught his face between her hands, kissing him with everything she couldn't say. When they broke apart, his eyes held the same fierce love she felt burning in her chest.

"Together?" she whispered.

"Together." He touched the ring on her finger. "In this life and the next."

Outside, Shadow Creek prepared for war. Ellie distributed weapons with practiced ease while Doctor Cooper prepared his surgery. The Apache warriors took their positions as storm clouds gathered above, promising thunder to match the coming guns.

And somewhere in the darkness, a trusted ally was sending signals to the enemy, proving that some betrayals cut deeper than bullets.

But for now, there was just this moment – two hearts beating in sync, two souls bound by something stronger than fate, and a love worth dying for.

Even if they had to die defending it.

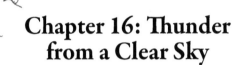

Chapter 16: Thunder from a Clear Sky

Dawn painted Shadow Creek in shades of blood and gold. Grace watched from the sheriff's office as Harris's men took position along Main Street, their numbers seeming to multiply like shadows at sunset.

"Ready for this?" Nate's voice was warm against her ear.

"Not even slightly." She turned in his arms. "Promise me something?"

"Anything."

"Don't die." Her attempt at lightness failed as her voice cracked.

His kiss tasted of gunpowder and promises. "Wouldn't dream of it. I have a wedding to attend."

The first shot came from the church tower – the signal they'd been waiting for. Harris's army poured into town like a flood, but Grace's people were ready.

Apache warriors emerged from hiding like spirits, their arrows finding marks with deadly precision. Ellie's voice rang out clear and sharp, directing defenders with military precision that surprised everyone except Doctor Cooper.

"Federal Marshal's office!" She called out, her badge catching morning light. "Surrender or—"

Gunfire cut her off, forcing her behind an overturned wagon where the doctor waited with his medical supplies.

"You know," he said conversationally as bullets splintered wood around them, "when I proposed, I was thinking more along the lines of a quiet ceremony."

"Boring." Ellie grinned, reloading her rifle. "This is much more romantic."

Grace lost track of time in the chaos that followed. She fought beside Nate like they'd been doing it forever, each movement synchronized, each shot complementing the other's.

Then she saw her father confronting Harris alone.

"It was you," Harris's voice cut through the gunfire. "You were supposed to die that night, Thomas. Really die."

"Sorry to disappoint." Grace's father stood his ground as Harris advanced. "I've always been bad at following orders."

"You could have had everything!" Harris's composure cracked. "Power, wealth, a legacy for your daughter—"

"I gave her something better." Thomas's eyes met Grace's across the street. "The truth."

The shot seemed to come from everywhere and nowhere. Grace watched in horror as her father stumbled, red blooming across his chest.

"Dad!"

She moved without thinking, but Nate caught her arm. "Grace, wait—"

"How touching." Harris emerged from the smoke, holding a familiar gun. "The whole family, together one last time."

More of his men appeared, surrounding them. Grace saw Ellie trying to signal something from her position, saw the Apache warriors regrouping in the shadows.

"You know what's funny?" Harris continued, his smile mad as a desert sun. "Your mother said almost the same thing. Right before she had her... accident."

"You bastard." Grace's gun was steady despite her rage.

"Now, now." Harris gestured, and two of his men dragged forward a struggling Nate. "Let's be civilized about this. After all, you have a choice to make."

Grace's heart stopped. The gun pressed to Nate's head left no doubt about the choice being offered.

"Don't," Nate's voice was steel. "Grace, don't you dare—"

"Shut up." Harris pressed his own gun to Thomas's wound, making him groan. "Here's the deal, Miss Wilson. Drop your weapon, surrender the badge, and I'll let them live. Resist, and... well."

Time seemed to freeze. Grace saw everything with crystal clarity – her father's blood staining the dirt, Nate's eyes fierce with love and determination, Ellie's subtle hand signals from behind the wagon.

She remembered their first kiss, their last night together, every promise whispered in darkness. Remembered her father's lessons about justice, her mother's diary full of secrets.

"You're right," she said finally. "I do have a choice."

Her gun moved before anyone could react. But who she aimed at, what happened next, would change everything.

Thunder cracked overhead in a cloudless sky, as if nature itself were holding its breath for what came next.

Grace's shot shattered the church bell, sending it crashing into Harris's men. The distraction was all the Apache warriors needed – arrows rained from every direction as Ellie's federal agents emerged from hiding.

"That's my girl," Nate grinned, taking advantage of his captors' surprise to break free.

Harris snarled, pressing his gun harder against Thomas's wound. "You really think you've won? I own this territory!"

"Not anymore." Grace's father's voice was weak but clear. "Show him, sweetheart."

Grace pulled her mother's diary from her vest. "Page forty-three, Vincent. The real land deeds. The ones showing who actually owns these mining rights."

Harris's face went white. "Those burned—"

"My wife was smarter than that." Thomas coughed, blood staining his lips. "She knew what you'd do. Knew you'd kill her. So she made copies. Lots of copies."

"You're bluffing."

"Try me." Grace kept her gun steady. "Drop it, Harris. It's over."

For a moment, she thought he would. Then his madness took over.

Everything happened at once. Harris swung his gun toward Grace. Nate shouted a warning. Thomas Wilson found one last surge of strength, throwing himself at Harris as the gun went off.

"Dad!" Grace's scream tore through the chaos.

Nate reached Harris first, his fist connecting with savage precision. But Harris was laughing even as he fell, blood on his teeth.

"Too late," he wheezed. "Always too late."

Grace reached her father as he collapsed. His blood was hot on her hands as she tried to stop the bleeding.

"Doctor!" Her voice broke. "Cooper!"

"Here." The doctor was already moving, his hands sure despite the ongoing battle around them. "Hold him still."

"Grace." Her father's grip was surprisingly strong. "The letter... in my boot..."

"Don't talk." She couldn't lose him. Not again. Not like this.

Nate appeared beside her, keeping watch while Ellie's agents secured the area. His free hand found her shoulder, steadying her.

"Stubborn... like your mother." Thomas smiled through the pain. "She'd be... so proud..."

"Stay with me." Grace clutched his hand. "Please, Daddy."

Thunder rolled across the desert as Doctor Cooper worked, his instruments glinting like hope in the chaos. The fate of everything – her father, her love, her town – hung balanced on a knife's edge.

And somewhere in the distance, a train whistle screamed like a promise or a curse, bringing with it changes that would reshape everything they knew.

But that was tomorrow's battle. Right now, there was just this moment – a father's blood on her hands, a lover's strength at her back, and a choice that would define not just her future, but the future of everything she loved.

The thunder cracked again, and Grace Wilson made her choice.

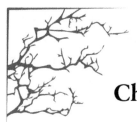

Chapter 17: In Fire

The train screamed into Shadow Creek like a demon from hell, belching smoke and carrying Harris's reinforcements. Grace had seconds to make her decision.

"Get everyone to the mine tunnels," she ordered Ellie. "Stage the wounded from there."

"And you?" Ellie's eyes were knowing.

"I'm finishing this." Grace checked her guns. "One way or another."

Doctor Cooper worked frantically over her father in the makeshift surgery they'd set up in the saloon's back room. Thomas Wilson's breathing was shallow, but his grip on Grace's hand remained strong.

"Go," he whispered. "End it."

"Dad—"

"That's an order, Deputy." His smile was weak but real. "Make it count."

Nate waited by the door, his expression grave. "Ready?"

"No." She kissed him hard, quick. "Watch your back."

"Always do." His eyes held promises. "Try not to shoot me this time."

"No promises."

They emerged into chaos. Harris's men poured from the train like ants from a disturbed hill, but the Apache warriors were ready. Arrows rained from concealed positions while Ellie's federal agents provided covering fire.

"Over there!" Nate pointed to where Harris was directing his men toward the mine entrance. "He's going for the documents!"

"Not this time." Grace's shot took out the lantern in Harris's hand. "You want those tunnels, Vincent? Come and get them."

Harris's laugh echoed through the smoke-filled street. "Always the hero, Miss Wilson. Just like your mother. Right up until the end."

"The difference is," Grace's voice carried clear and cold, "I know exactly what you are."

The battle flowed into the mine tunnels like water finding its level. Gunshots echoed off stone walls, creating a deafening cacophony. Grace lost track of Nate in the chaos, but caught glimpses of Ellie directing survivors deeper into the tunnels where Sarah waited with supplies.

"You think you've won?" Harris's voice bounced off the walls, impossible to locate. "Your father's dying. Your lover's outnumbered. Your precious town is burning. And for what? Justice?"

A shot grazed Grace's arm. She rolled behind a support beam, returning fire.

"Actually," she called back, "I just really don't like you."

Nate's laugh came from somewhere to her left, followed by precise shots that dropped two of Harris's men.

The mine groaned ominously. Someone had set charges – the whole place could come down at any moment.

"Grace!" Ellie's voice echoed urgently. "Your father—"

But the rest was lost as Harris emerged from the shadows, holding a detonator.

"One last choice, Deputy." His smile was mad as a desert sun. "The documents that'll destroy me, or the lives of everyone in these tunnels. Tick tock."

Movement caught her eye – Nate circling behind Harris, silent as a shadow. But Harris must have seen something in her face.

He spun, firing. Nate went down hard.

"No!" Grace's scream tore from her throat.

"Always too late," Harris laughed. "Like mother, like daughter."

But he'd made a crucial mistake – taking his eyes off the other tunnel entrance. Thomas Wilson appeared like a ghost, pale but standing, Doctor Cooper supporting him.

"Not this time." Her father's shot was perfect, knocking the detonator from Harris's hand.

Grace didn't hesitate. Her bullet took Harris in the shoulder, spinning him into the wall. But he was still laughing as he fell.

"The charges," he gasped. "Already set. Two minutes... maybe less..."

"Everybody out!" Grace shouted, running to Nate. "Now!"

"Just a scratch," Nate grunted as she helped him up. "Though my dramatic timing could use work."

"Your everything could use work." But she was smiling through tears.

They emerged into sunlight just as the first explosion rocked the mine. Harris's laughter turned to screams as the tunnel collapsed, burying his secrets and sins in darkness.

Grace found her father in Doctor Cooper's surgery, barely conscious but still fighting.

"The town?" he whispered.

"Standing." She took his hand. "Thanks to you."

"Thanks to us." His grip was weak but present. "Your mother would be..." His eyes closed.

"Dad?" Fear clutched her heart.

"He's stabilizing," Cooper said quickly. "But the next few hours..."

Nate found her later in the surgery's back room, bandaged but whole. His kiss tasted of smoke and survival and promises.

"Thought I'd lost you," she whispered against his mouth.

"Never." He pulled her closer, mindful of both their injuries. "Though next time, let's skip the explosions."

"Where's the fun in that?"

93

Their laughter was fragile but real. Outside, Shadow Creek began the work of rebuilding as Ellie's federal agents secured what was left of Harris's men.

Sarah appeared in the doorway, looking battered but determined. "There's something you need to see. Both of you."

But whatever revelations waited could wait a moment longer. Right now, there was just this – two hearts beating in sync, two souls who'd walked through fire and emerged stronger, and a love that had survived every test fate could devise.

The rest was just details.

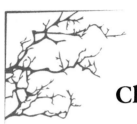

Chapter 18: Dawn

Chapter 18: Dawn

Shadow Creek bloomed like a desert flower after rain. Three months after the battle, new buildings rose from the ashes, stronger than before. The railroad still came – progress was inevitable – but on the town's terms, not Harris's.

Grace stood at her office window, watching the sunrise paint the street gold. Her father's badge – now officially hers – caught the light as she pinned it to her wedding dress.

"Having second thoughts about marrying an outlaw?" Thomas Wilson's voice was strong again, though he still walked with a cane.

"Former outlaw." She turned, smiling. "Former marshal. Former lot of things."

"Current pain in my side," he grumbled, but his eyes were bright. "Ready?"

The church had been rebuilt first, its new bells donated by the Apache tribe. Sarah had outdone herself with the decorations, white roses and desert wildflowers transforming the sanctuary.

"Last chance to run," Ellie teased as she helped with Grace's veil. The former saloon owner – now officially Special Agent Martinez-Cooper – was radiant in her own recent wedded bliss.

"And miss seeing Nate in a proper suit? Never."

But when she saw him waiting at the altar, Grace forgot about propriety entirely. His eyes lit up like sunrise, and suddenly they were back in that saloon, pointing guns at each other, neither knowing they'd just met their destiny.

"Dearly beloved," Father Michael began, then paused as Nate failed to hide his grin. "Is something amusing, Mr. Blackwood?"

"Just remembering the last time we were all in this church," Nate's eyes danced. "Considerably more shooting involved."

"If you're expecting gunfire at my wedding," Grace warned, "I'm starting with you."

"I'd expect nothing less, love."

Their vows were unconventional – promises of partnership mixed with playful threats, declarations of love woven with shared memories of danger and triumph. When Nate slipped his mother's ring onto her finger, his hands trembled slightly.

"I promise to always watch your back," he said softly.

"And I promise to always call you on your nonsense," she returned, making the congregation laugh.

The celebration spilled into the newly rebuilt Golden Horseshoe, where Ellie had outdone herself. The Apache chief presented them with ceremonial blankets, while Doctor Cooper raised a toast that had everyone wiping eyes.

"To those who couldn't be here," he said, meeting Grace's gaze, "but who led us to where we needed to be."

Grace's father caught her hand as the dancing began. "Your mother would be proud," he said softly. "Of everything you've done. Everything you've become."

"Everything we've done," she corrected, hugging him. The past wasn't forgotten, but it was forgiven. Family, she'd learned, was too precious to waste on old hurts.

"May I cut in?" Nate appeared, looking devastating in his formal suit. "Promise to return her relatively unscathed, sir."

"Like you could keep her from trouble if you tried," Thomas snorted, but his smile was warm as he handed Grace over.

They moved together like they'd been dancing all their lives, just as they'd fought together, loved together, built something beautiful from the ashes of the past.

"Happy?" Nate murmured against her hair.

"Deliriously." She tilted her face up to his. "Though I notice you're still armed under that fancy suit."

"So are you."

"Well," she smiled against his mouth, "a girl needs her accessories."

Later, as stars painted the desert sky with silver, they slipped away from the celebration. Their new house waited on the edge of town – a wedding gift from the grateful citizens of Shadow Creek.

"Welcome home, Mrs. Blackwood," Nate whispered, carrying her across the threshold.

"That's Sheriff Blackwood to you," she corrected, then lost her train of thought as his kiss turned heated.

They came together with the passion of their first time and the tenderness of knowing every inch of each other by heart. Moonlight painted silver patterns on their skin as they celebrated their own private ceremony of love and promise.

Dawn found them on their balcony, watching the sun paint their town in shades of hope. Shadow Creek was changing, growing, but its heart remained true – like the love that had saved it.

"So," Nate's arms wrapped around her waist, "ready for new adventures?"

"With you?" She leaned back against him, feeling his heart beat in time with hers. "Always."

A rider appeared on the horizon, carrying what looked like an urgent message. Grace felt Nate tense expectantly behind her.

"Duty calls, Sheriff?"

She turned in his arms, kissing him with all the love and promise of their shared future. "Care to ride with me, partner?"

His smile was as bright as the rising sun. "Lead the way, love. Lead the way."

And so they rode out together, into whatever adventure waited beyond the horizon. Because some loves are written in gunsmoke and starlight, some destinies forged in fire and faith.

And sometimes, the greatest adventure of all is simply coming home to the heart that knows yours best.

Don't miss out!

Visit the website below and you can sign up to receive emails whenever Beate Lang publishes a new book. There's no charge and no obligation.

https://books2read.com/r/B-A-SNURC-TNIFF

BOOKS 2 READ

Connecting independent readers to independent writers.

About the Author

Beate Lang grew up surrounded by the tales of the Wild West that fascinated her German town. With a degree in history and a deep love for the stories of strength and survival, she began writing novels that bring the rugged allure of the frontier to life. Helga's works are known for their rich character dynamics, unexpected twists, and vivid scenes that place readers right in the heart of an untamed land. When she's not writing, she enjoys horseback riding, exploring remote landscapes, and uncovering lesser-known historical tales. Beate Lang's novels invite readers to a world where honor is everything and love is won through fire and grit.

Milton Keynes UK
Ingram Content Group UK Ltd.
UKHW021123111124
451035UK00016B/1178